"If We're Going To Work Together, We Need To Forget Tonight Ever Happened."

"Why's that?" Joe asked.

"Isn't it obvious?"

"Apparently only to you, Arianna. The way I see it, we reached out to each other. We kissed. We made love. It felt good. It felt great. Didn't it feel great?"

"Yes, but—"

"No buts. We needed each other. We met those needs. We're adults." Joe was silent for several seconds, then finally said, "You can try to ignore it all you want. I choose not to."

"Meaning what?"

"I'm not going to ignore it. Or forget it. It meant something to me. Didn't it mean anything to you?"

How was she supposed to answer that? Damn him.

Dear Reader,

Welcome to another passion-filled month at Silhouette Desire—where we guarantee powerful and provocative love stories you are sure to enjoy. We continue our fabulous DYNASTIES: THE DANFORTHS series with Kristi Gold's *Challenged by the Sheikh*—her intensely ardent hero will put your senses on overload. More hot heroes are on the horizon when *USA TODAY* bestselling author Ann Major returns to Silhouette Desire with the dramatic story of *The Bride Tamer*.

Ever wonder what it would be like to be a man's mistress— even just for pretend? Well, the heroine of Katherine Garbera's *Mistress Minded* finds herself just in that predicament when she agrees to help out her sexy-as-sin boss in the next KING OF HEARTS title. Jennifer Greene brings us the second story in THE SCENT OF LAVENDER, her compelling series about the Campbell sisters, with *Wild In the Moonlight*—and this is one hero to go wild for! If it's a heartbreaker you're looking for, look no farther than *Hold Me Tight* by Cait London as she continues her HEARTBREAKERS miniseries with this tale of one sexy male specimen on the loose. And looking for a little *Hot Contact* himself is the hero of Susan Crosby's latest book in her BEHIND CLOSED DOORS series; this sinfully seductive police investigator always gets his woman! Thank goodness.

And thank *you* for coming back to Silhouette Desire every month. Be sure to join us next month for *New York Times* bestselling author Lisa Jackson's *Best-Kept Lies,* the highly anticipated conclusion to her wildly popular series THE McCAFFERTYS.

Keep on reading!

Melissa Jeglinski

Melissa Jeglinski
Senior Editor, Silhouette Desire

Please address questions and book requests to:
Silhouette Reader Service
U.S.: 3010 Walden Ave., P.O. Box 1325, Buffalo, NY 14269
Canadian: P.O. Box 609, Fort Erie, Ont. L2A 5X3

HOT CONTACT
SUSAN CROSBY

Silhouette®
Desire

Published by Silhouette Books
America's Publisher of Contemporary Romance

SILHOUETTE BOOKS

ISBN 0-373-76590-8

HOT CONTACT

Visit Silhouette Books at www.eHarlequin.com

Printed in U.S.A.

Books by Susan Crosby

Silhouette Desire

The Mating Game #888
Almost a Honeymoon #952
Baby Fever #1018
Wedding Fever #1061
Marriage on His Mind #1108
Bride Candidate #9 #1131
*His Most Scandalous Secret #1158
*His Seductive Revenge #1162
*His Ultimate Temptation #1186
The Groom's Revenge #1214
The Baby Gift #1301
†Christmas Bonus, Strings Attached #1554
†Private Indiscretions #1570
†Hot Contact #1590

*The Lone Wolves
†Behind Closed Doors

_____

SUSAN CROSBY

believes in the value of setting goals, but also in the
magic of making wishes. A longtime reader of romance
novels, Susan earned a B.A. in English while raising her
sons. She lives in the central valley of California, the
land of wine grapes, asparagus and almonds. Her check-
ered past includes jobs as a synchronized swimming
instructor, personnel interviewer at a toy factory and
trucking company manager, but her current occupation
as a writer is her all-time favorite.

Susan enjoys writing about people who take a chance on
love, sometimes against all odds. She loves warm, strong
heroes; good-hearted, self-reliant heroines…and happy
endings.

Readers are welcome to write to her at P.O. Box 1836,
Lodi, CA 95241.

For Jerry, who patiently answers my questions and
makes me look smart!

And for Jack—because.

One

Joe Vicente strode into his office and stumbled over a body pierced with half a dozen daggers. He studied the giant of a man sprawled on the floor, then he did what any veteran homicide detective would do—he laughed. Small Corn Flakes boxes were stuck to the man's chest, knife handles protruding from each box. Unnatural red blood dripped from the points of entry.

"You get it?" the body asked.

Joe got it. "Cereal killer. Good one, Reggie." He walked backward toward his desk. "You going trick-or-treating on your way home?"

"Nah. I'm meeting the wife at the Blue Zoo for a Halloween party. Wanna come?"

"No, thanks. If I'm not there to pass out candy to the little monsters, they egg the house."

Reggie straightened his costume as he stood. "I didn't think kids did that anymore."

"They do in my neighborhood." Joe turned around and bumped into a descendent of Al Capone, wearing a pin-striped suit, black shirt, white tie and Fedora. Tony Mendes, the newest detective assigned to the elite Robbery-Homicide Division of the Los Angeles Police Department—and Joe's partner.

Joe grinned. He couldn't remember a Halloween in his seven years in RHD when anyone had dressed up. But then the Blue Zoo, the local cop watering hole, had just changed ownership, expanded and was making an effort to draw a bigger crowd.

Joe dropped his notebook onto his desk and spied Lieutenant Morgan heading his way.

"Interview room two, Vicente," he said to Joe. "Now."

The lieutenant's tone of voice said Joe wasn't being invited to a party.

He avoided eye contact with the other detectives as he followed Morgan. In the interview room he sat in the chair across the table from the lieutenant, slouched a little and crossed his ankles. His stomach caught fire, but he didn't reach for the antacid tablets he chewed like candy, not in front of the boss.

Morgan leaned back, stone-faced. At six foot two, he was as tall as Joe but had ten years and thirty pounds on him. Morgan was a good supervisor. Fair. "Catch me up on the Leventhal case."

"Dead ends. One after another."

The lieutenant was quiet long enough to almost make Joe squirm. He knew the tactic, *used* the tactic. Shut up and the let other person bear the burden of the silence, forcing them to speak first.

"I've cleared you for four weeks' vacation," Morgan said, his gaze steady.

Shock rolled through Joe in tidal waves. He fought to

maintain his equilibrium. Vacation, hell. He'd lost his cool too many times lately, but the last thing he needed was a vacation. Time on his hands? No way. "I know you're not happy with my work—"

Morgan frowned. "It's got nothing to do with your work, Joe. You're a damn good cop. But you are this close to being reassigned. *This close.*" A piece of paper might have fit between his thumb and index finger. "That's about a day from now."

"I can't go on vacation."

"You need to get away from here. Right now. Before you get hurt, before someone else gets hurt. Never mind that you've worked the Leventhal case way too long. It should've been filed by now."

"I can't get the witnesses to cooperate. You know that."

"Yeah, and you're taking it out on everyone here. When you walked in just now, that's the most civil any of us has seen you for months. You don't think the captain hasn't noticed? I'm saving your hide here. You start vacation tomorrow."

Desperation slammed into him. His lungs froze. If he didn't have work, he wouldn't survive. The constant burning in his gut would only get worse. He didn't want to think about what it would do to his insomnia.

"Two weeks," Joe countered. Maybe he could tolerate two weeks.

"Four. And if anyone sees you at the site of the Leventhal shooting or hears you're trying to contact a witness, you won't have a desk to come back to."

Joe knew Morgan was right. Something had to change. But staying away from the job wasn't the solution. Legally they couldn't force him to use his vacation time, either.

"You know I can't leave town," he said. It was as close to begging as he would get.

"Maybe that's exactly what you need," the lieutenant said, his voice not as gritty. "How long has it been since you went away? Since you went on a date, even? I know you've been through hell, but take the time and be grateful for it. Clear your head. Take back your life."

"Or don't come back?"

Morgan crossed his arms. "I want the case file and notes on my desk before you leave tonight."

Joe was thirty-nine years old and an eighteen-year veteran of the LAPD. He knew a dismissal when he heard one. He also knew not to argue with the boss, especially one who thought he was doing you a favor.

"Who'll take over on Leventhal?"

"Mendes."

Joe tried not to wince. "He's green."

"As green as you were seven years ago. You solved your share of cases from the beginning."

Joe stayed at his desk for an hour organizing his notes. No one would call him at home with questions, even if he didn't include every detail he knew, but he covered all the bases regardless. Mendes knew most everything anyway.

Everyone but the lieutenant was gone by the time Joe put the folder on Morgan's desk.

"Thanks," he said. "See you after Thanksgiving."

Joe nodded, started to leave then turned back. His jaw ached from clenching his teeth. At least Morgan knew he hadn't slacked off, that he'd continued to give his best to the job, even when he wasn't coping well with the frustration of dead ends. And life.

"Call me with me a progress report now and then," Morgan said.

"Yeah." He left, the effort to walk almost more than he could manage. Now what? Go home and face the demanding trick-or-treaters? It would be easier to scrape dried, splattered eggs off his house.

Go to the Blue Zoo and forget himself in the booze and shoptalk? Given his mood, he'd probably end up in a fight.

He made his way to his car. On the passenger seat was an invitation he'd been carrying around for a couple of weeks. He picked it up. A costume party thrown by Scott Simons, his training officer after graduation from the academy. When Scott retired twelve years ago, he became a lawyer and had built a reputation for winning tough criminal cases. The Halloween party was at his house in Santa Monica and would start in an hour.

Costume and mask required. Joe drummed his fingers on his steering wheel. He wasn't a costume kind of guy. But if he went to Scott's party he would be among strangers mostly, hot-shot lawyers and a celebrity client or two. He'd be anonymous, but not alone. It was better than the alternatives, especially staying home and drinking himself into oblivion, which was the last thing his stomach needed.

Take back your life. Lieutenant Morgan's words jabbed him.

He tossed the invitation onto the seat, started the engine and pulled out of his parking spot. He couldn't believe he was asking himself this question, but where could he find a decent costume at six o'clock on Halloween night? Something a little more original than a George W. Bush mask. Something without a ruffled shirt or that required him to say, "Yeah, baby," all night.

Surreal, Joe thought, shaking his head. Utterly surreal. He would've laughed—had it been the least bit funny.

The party was in full swing, the music loud and the party goers boisterous—exactly the kind of gathering that Arianna Alvarado loved. Crowds and noise were an invigorating change from her relatively quiet work life. She sipped her martini, appreciating the bite of the gin, then drew a green olive into her mouth and chewed it. "You're sure he's not coming?" she asked the man standing next to her.

"I told you it was a long shot at best," Scott Simons answered. They stood in the foyer as Scott greeted arriving guests. "If he can't wear jeans and boots, he's not going to show."

"Add a western shirt and a Stetson, and you've got a classic," Arianna pointed out.

"But still a costume."

Arianna shrugged her agreement. "He didn't say no, though?"

"If he were coming, he would've called."

Disappointment twisted a knot in her anticipation, choking it off.

Scott welcomed a couple dressed as pro wrestlers then pointed them toward the bar. "Why don't you just call him at the P.D.?" he asked Arianna.

"It doesn't suit my purposes."

He turned to her, his brows raised, a smile flickering. "So you weren't telling me the truth when you asked me to include him on the guest list. It's personal, not business."

"It's business, in a personal way," she offered, along with a smile. The business was her own.

"He likes beautiful women. He would like you a lot, Arianna."

"Flatterer," she said in return. She didn't want Detective Joe Vicente of the LAPD to like her, however. The one time they'd met, last December, she'd felt a pull toward him that seemed reciprocated, but he hadn't followed up on it. Neither had she. Mutual attraction. Mutual reluctance.

She'd been glad then. He would've been hard to say no to, but she definitely would've said no.

"Have I told you how stunning you look in that flamenco costume?" Scott eyed the large red rose tucked behind her ear in her low-coiled hair. He winked. "I wouldn't mind a private performance."

She gave him a sultry look—or she hoped it was sultry, but she was wearing a mask, so she wasn't sure he could tell. She knew he had no interest in a private performance; he had a beautiful wife whom he adored. But Arianna raised an arm anyway, assumed a classic dance pose and clicked her castanets above her head. Her ruffled skirt brushed her knees in front and her ankles in back. She'd wanted to draw Detective Vicente's attention tonight. A wasted effort now.

With a laugh she tugged on Scott's long white barrister's wig then walked away, wandering out to the backyard bar by the pool, stopping here and there to talk with other guests as she went. She had the bartender add another toothpick full of olives to the drink she would baby all evening, then went in search of a quiet spot to consider her next move. How could she get Joe Vicente's unofficial help?

She moved along a path around the pool, past the cabana and into a dense profusion of fragrant vegetation, following the sound of trickling water to its source—a rock waterfall in a hidden grotto, humid and verdant.

She stopped when she saw a man dressed in black standing next to the falls, lost in his own world, a tall, lean man with dark hair, wearing high boots, snug pants, loosely flowing shirt and a dashing hat, tipped forward rakishly. A mask hid half his face. Zorro. He carried himself well, his posture perfect, with a hint of the arrogance Zorro was

known for. She expected him to draw his sword and slash
a Z in the air at any moment.

Intrigued, Arianna straightened her satin mask and took
a step toward him. Perhaps the evening wouldn't be a complete waste, after all.

Joe's nose twitched as a spicy scent assaulted him then
radiated to the far reaches of his body, creating a sudden,
intense heat. He searched for the fragrant flower source but
saw instead a woman approaching him—tall and dark-
haired, with a body better than dreams could usually con-
jure up. Her costume was exotic-looking. Skinny straps,
low cut, fitting each amazing curve snugly and ending in
ruffles that undulated with every step. Long legs, high
heels. Red and black, satin and lace. A rose behind her ear.
Red lips. A small beauty mark at the corner of her mouth.
Black mask trimmed in lace. Dark, unfathomable eyes behind it.

She looked like sex, if it had a human name.

"Buenos noches," she said with a perfect accent, her
teeth white against the red lipstick.

"Buenos noches." He guessed her age as thirty. She
wasn't wearing a ring.

"May I join you?" she asked.

He held out a hand to help her negotiate the final steps
leading to the substantial rock ledge where he stood. Her
breasts were covered only by a layer of smooth lace, her
nipples pressing against the fabric. He managed to shift his
focus to her face as she pulled her hand free.

"Thank you," she said, then looked around. "This is
beautiful, isn't it? I hope I'm not interrupting."

"You are. Thank you."

She smiled.

Joe tried to place her. There was something familiar

about her. Her voice? Her body? With that kind of self-assurance, an actress, he decided. Could he have seen her in a movie? Joe knew most of the criminal attorneys in the L.A. area. None of them looked like her. If she would take off her mask…

"So, you're not wearing your cape, Zorro," the woman said.

"It's not a black-tie event."

Her laugh was light and musical and seemed to have magic powers. The burn in his stomach cooled to a simmer. "Do you dance?" he asked.

"Doesn't everyone?"

"I mean as you're dressed—flamenco." He wanted to see her in motion, to smell her spicy perfume as her body heated up. It had been so long since he'd felt anything remotely close to lust, he almost didn't recognize the signs—how his breathing turned shallow and his pulse pounded and his body went on alert, as if a caution sign had been placed in front of him, a sign he wanted to plow through. Caution be damned.

"I dance," she said, confidence in the lift of her chin, the move emphasizing her slender neck.

He waited. She didn't offer to perform. Tension hovered between them, although it was more anticipation than uneasiness.

"How do you know Scott?" she asked, breaking the silence.

He'd started to get swept into a fantasy. Her question brought him back to earth. "Professionally. You?"

"The same."

That nagging sense of familiarity returned. Had Scott defended her? A case that generated media attention?

She gestured toward the path leading back to the pool area. "I think perhaps I interrupted you, after all," she said, her expression as apologetic as her mask would allow. "I'll go."

"No." He caught her by the hand then didn't release her. He hadn't realized how little he'd spoken. Obviously he had made her uncomfortable. "I had a rough day." Week. Month. Year. "I thought I dreamed you up."

Her dark gaze held him captive. "I'm quite real."

"I can see that." He didn't know what else to say. She was like a beacon in the fog of his world. He wanted to follow the light, to let it shine on him, to brighten his existence. Pure selfishness, he admitted, since he had nothing to offer her or any woman except dead emotions, a screwed-up mind, an ulcer, probably, and the short fuse of a man long deprived of uninterrupted sleep. Plus a job in jeopardy. Oh, yeah. He had a lot going for him, all right.

Take back your life. Again the lieutenant's words assaulted him. Suddenly he wanted his life back. No, not back, but better.

The woman continued to study him. He didn't break eye contact. Couldn't. Something about her demanded that he look deeply into her eyes, to allow her to look into his, not an easy feat with masks on. Finally she set her martini glass aside and took a step toward him.

"Dance?" she asked, soft and low, as music filtered in from hidden speakers.

He took her into his arms. Her body felt lithe and limber as they moved to the slow rhythm. He pulled the rose from her hair and dragged it across her cheek. Her eyes glittered darkly. He went hard with need.

One strap of her sexy dress slid off her shoulder and down her arm. He hooked a finger into the fallen strap and dragged it onto her shoulder. She didn't protest nor did she encourage him toward more. He let his finger slide down the strap until it met fabric. Her breast cushioned his hand;

he felt her breath stop then tugged her toward him, his gaze on hers, lowered his head, brought his mouth close—

"Well. I see you've met," Scott Simons said into the magic moment.

Joe swore.

Two

The stranger's single, explicit curse flattered Arianna, but before she could decide why, he took a step back from her. Regret and relief assaulted her simultaneously. She was aroused, more than she'd been in a long time, and she'd known him for ten minutes! She should be grateful that Scott had come along....

But she wasn't.

"Everyone has unmasked," Scott said, grinning as if something momentous was about to happen.

Arianna glanced at the man dressed as Zorro. Would he take off his mask? He seemed reluctant—or maybe he was still caught up in what they'd just experienced. She'd danced with him because she'd recognized something even his mask couldn't hide—a kindred spirit. Battle weariness. Like her. So they'd distracted each other from whatever demons haunted them.

Arianna lifted her mask away. He seemed to stop

breathing. She saw his eyes close for longer than a blink, then he took off his hat and untied his mask.

"Yes, we've met," he said to Scott, but looking at her. "Ms. Alvarado. It's nice to see you again."

She wanted to punch Scott in the mouth. Anything to wipe that stupid grin off his face. "Detective," she said calmly to the man she'd come to the party hoping to see. "How've you been?"

"Business, my ass," Scott said before he left them alone.

"What was that supposed to mean?" Joe asked.

"Does anyone know why Scott says the things he does?" she replied, her fists clenched. She ran a few sentences through her head. Everything sounded inane. "Well," she began.

One corner of his mouth lifted. "That was interesting."

Her shoulders loosened. "'Interesting' tells me nothing."

"Care to put your spin on it?"

She settled on honesty, especially since she had a favor to ask of him. "I don't usually come on that strong."

His brows lifted as if he didn't quite believe her. He tucked her rose back in her hair. His fingertips grazed her ear then her neck, his gaze serious. "Thank you for the dance."

She shivered. Annoyance came hard and fast. What was going on? She knew how to control her reaction but made no effort to. That attraction she'd felt last December was as strong as ever. "You're welcome."

She wanted to ask him why he'd come, since Scott had been adamant that Joe wouldn't dress for Halloween. "I like your choice of costume," she said.

"I can't wait to take it off. How about you?"

She swallowed the innuendo that sprang to mind. "I'm comfortable in mine." She couldn't be alone with him for one more minute. She'd never been so unguardedly drawn to anyone, ever. If she wanted his help, she needed to stay businesslike, to act like the thirty-three-year-old professional woman she was, not some hormonal teenager. "Shall we head back to the party?"

"All right," he said, although with surprise on his face. "I take it your firm has done work for Scott?"

"For a number of years." She led the way down the path toward the pool. She'd been a private investigator for seven years. Her company, ARC Security & Investigations, did consulting and investigative work for many attorneys in the area, especially on high-profile cases.

"I met him eighteen years ago," Joe said. "He was my training officer after I graduated from the academy. We stayed in touch for a long time." They emerged from the trail. "Although I hadn't seen him in a couple of years. He's been busy."

"I see him more on television than in the office these days, too," she said, eyeing the crowd mingling around the pool. She didn't want to ask her favor tonight at the party. She also didn't dare leave him alone, since Scott might decide to tell him she'd specifically requested he be invited.

Now what? She couldn't leave until he did. And she couldn't wander away. Small talk?

"Do you know anyone else here?" she asked.

"No. Did you come alone?"

I wanted to see you. "Yes."

"That surprises me." He gestured to a couple of chaise lounges. "We should grab those while they're empty. Can I get you a drink?"

She'd left hers behind at the waterfall, she realized. "Yes, please. Martini with a twist, extra olives."

"I'll be right back."

She'd barely settled on a lounge when Scott sat down on the one next to hers.

"Did you know he was here?" she asked, watching Joe talk to the bartender.

Scott looked at her over his wineglass, then took a sip. "Yes."

"Is that how you entertain yourself?"

"You're a cool one, aren't you, Arianna?" He settled a little more comfortably. "Controlled. Smart. I'd never seen you ruffled by anything until you found out I knew Joe."

"It was a simple favor to ask, inviting him to the party," she said, wishing she had her drink already, needing the prop.

"More than that, I think."

She hesitated. Joe was walking toward them. "You won't say anything."

"I don't know how this is going to play out." He smiled, patted her knee and stood, making room for Joe, leaning to whisper in her ear, "You know he's not engaged anymore, right?"

Arianna said nothing. She didn't know he *had* been engaged. Was that the reason for the battle-weary look in his eyes? Had he broken it off or had his fiancée?

She thanked Joe as he passed her the drink then raised her brows at Scott, indicating he could move on.

Scott grinned. "So, how do you two know each other?"

"We met during Alexis Wells's attempted murder last year," Arianna said, aware of Joe taking a seat beside her and stretching out those long legs. His knee-high black Zorro boots made her smile. "Joe was the detective in charge of the case."

"You worked together? The cop and the P.I.? Strange bedfellows." He met Arianna's gaze and smiled benignly.

"We shared information without insulting each other's profession," Joe said. "She's a cut above in her field."

"Yeah. Most P.I.s only get to eat what they kill," Scott responded. "But not Arianna and her partners."

"We work hard." Her irritation grew. She'd always had a great business relationship with Scott. Why was he making things difficult for her now?

"Scott," Joe said, his voice quiet but firm. "I like you. But if you continue to offend Ms. Alvarado, she's going to leave. And I'm not going to like you anymore."

A few seconds ticked by, then Scott lifted his glass to Joe. "To the thrill of the chase."

Joe stared back.

"Thanks," Arianna said when their host walked away.

Joe shrugged. "Sometimes he doesn't know when to quit."

"I've noticed." She slid a green olive off the toothpick and sucked on it. "Pushing the right buttons is what makes him good in the courtroom, though."

"But lousy as a friend sometimes." Joe leaned toward her. "Would you like to get out of here? Go somewhere quiet?"

She was tempted. Entirely too tempted. But if she accepted his invitation she couldn't move the relationship into a business one when she needed to. She had no intention of lying to him or stringing him along. She just didn't want to ask her favor publicly—or in costume. It was too serious for that. The party had been a way to open a dialogue. "I'd love a rain check," she said.

He studied her for a long time. She made herself breathe.

"Walk me to my car and I'll give you my number," he said, standing. "You can call me when the sun comes out."

She smiled. "All right."

Joe offered her a hand up. He was probably crazy to

pursue her. He should at least wait until his life was back on track, yet he couldn't help but feel she was part of the solution. Wishful thinking, maybe?

They made their way through the crowded house. He guided her slightly ahead of him with a touch to her lower back, just enough to feel the bones of her vertebrae against his fingertips now and then. She turned and looked at him once, her dark eyes again taking his measure in a way no woman in his memory had. She looked deeply, as she had by the waterfall, without blinking. Did he meet her standards or pass her test or whatever it was she was doing when she looked at him like that?

They reached his SUV. He got a business card out of his glove compartment, wrote his home and cell numbers on the back and passed it to her.

"Something on your mind?" he asked when she said nothing. He curled his fingers into his palms, resisting touching her. He wondered how long her hair was. A year ago it was just past her shoulders.

"You're different from other detectives," she said. "I noticed that before."

"Different, how?"

"Quieter."

"And not intimidated?"

She smiled. "Do I intimidate?"

"Competence is often intimidating."

Arms folded, she leaned a hip and shoulder against his passenger door. "I think I've been complimented."

"You have."

"You impress me as well."

"I'm glad to hear that." He moved closer, crowding her space a little.

She didn't budge, not even when he slipped a finger under her strap as he had by the waterfall. He focused on the little beauty mark at the corner of her mouth. "This is very pretty," he said, kissing the spot. He felt her lips part, heard a soft sound, more than a breath catching, less than surrender. He moved his mouth over hers lightly, brushing his lips against hers, pulling back, making her come to him.

A horn honked. Teenage boys shouted crude encouragement. The only encouragement Joe needed was Arianna's. When he wouldn't take the kiss any deeper she placed her hands along his face and held him still.

"You tease," she said, her voice husky.

"Just making sure of my welcome."

Her hesitation lasted all of two seconds. "The door's open."

He wanted to skim his hands over her incredible body, to feel the weight of her breasts, the curve of her hips, the firm fullness of her rear. He settled for a long, leisurely kiss that she kept trying to deepen and he kept thwarting. He knew he had to leave her wanting more or she wouldn't call him, so he gave her enough to think about but not to satisfy. Gave himself a lot to think about, too, like what it would be like to make love, a foreign concept to him in the past six months.

He pulled back. She opened her eyes. Her skin was drawn taut over her cheekbones. He let his gaze wander lower as she watched. Her nipples were hard. She arched her back just enough that he noticed the unspoken invitation to touch. He declined, counting on there being another time and a better place.

"*Adios,*" he said, forcing himself to leave her. He walked around his car and got in, then didn't look back until he was far enough away that she couldn't see him glance in his rearview mirror.

She wasn't staring after him, however, but was strolling

back up to Scott's house, her hips swaying, the ruffled hem intoxicating in its undulating rhythm. She didn't glance in his direction.

After a moment he smiled. He'd met his match.

Three

Arianna tapped Joe's business card against her thigh as she stared out her living room window at the typical hazy Southern California morning. She had his home number. Why procrastinate?

Dumb question. Because of last night, that's why. Because of the kiss. The almost-as-good-as-sex kiss. How could she ask him to help her now? He would think she kissed him to get him interested, to lure him so that he would cooperate. Nothing was further from the truth. She'd gotten carried away—rare for her.

She was also hesitating because she hadn't yet recovered from last night's nightmare, the one that had been haunting her for weeks. The one that had spurred her toward Joe Vicente.

Arianna turned from the window and sat at her piano, a shiny, black baby grand that dominated her apartment living room. She tapped out a few random notes, then eased into scales. When her fingers were limber, she played a piece she'd composed, a complex, demanding song still being refined.

After playing the final chord, she sat up straight, set her hands on her thighs and enjoyed the quiet for a moment. Then she talked to herself.

Okay, stall over. Bite the bullet.

She grabbed the portable phone and dialed. He answered on the third ring.

"Good morning, it's Arianna Alvarado," she said, as businesslike as possible.

"Good morning back," he replied, a sound suspiciously like laughter in his voice. "And thank you for being specific. It could've been embarrassing if I had you confused with the other Arianna."

Oh, he knew how he affected her. "The sun hasn't broken through," she said, forging ahead, "but I'm inviting you to lunch anyway."

"Don't trust yourself to have dinner with me?"

The underlying sensuality in his voice appealed to her way too much. She started pacing. "Yes."

"Yes, you don't trust yourself?"

"Yes, I trust myself, but I'm inviting you to lunch."

"Sorry, but I'm headed to my parents' house. I expect to be there all afternoon."

Her heart slammed into her chest. Even better. She could meet his father. Talk to him. "Can I meet you there?" she asked.

A long silence, then, "At my parents' house?"

"Yes."

"I don't usually bring a woman home until the tenth date."

Like your ex-fiancée? "Will you make an exception?"

Silence again. "Sure, why not?" He gave her the address and directions.

"I have to make a stop first," she said. "Can I bring lunch with me?"

"That'd be great, thanks."

"Is there anything I shouldn't bring? Allergic to shellfish or anything?"

"No allergies here."

"Okay. I'll see you in a couple of hours." She hung up then went in search of something to wear to meet his parents. His father. A man she'd never met, a man whose name she didn't know until a month ago, but whom she'd hated for twenty-five years.

Arianna pulled into a circular driveway of an impressive Spanish Colonial mansion and parked near the garage. She bypassed the front door to jog down a side path into the backyard where she saw several linen-covered round tables with umbrellas set up near the large, tiled swimming pool. The view of the Hollywood Hills was incredible.

She spotted her mother twining elegant leaf garlands around the umbrella poles. Arianna forgot what today's event was. A fashion show, perhaps? Something to raise money for a worthy cause, probably. That was what her mother did for a living ever since she'd married Estebán Clemente, international movie mogul, when Arianna was twelve.

Estebán had changed their lives in immeasurable ways. But one topic was never brought up for discussion—Arianna's father.

"Mom!" she called.

Paloma Alvarado Clemente never hurried. She carried herself with grace and dignity, her skin and make-up flawless, her striking silver and black hair styled in a fashionable bob. She wore brightly colored designer clothing, and jewelry that clinked and clanked—a striking silver necklace and bracelets crafted by artisans from her native Mexico.

Paloma waited for Arianna now, a serene smile on her face, her arms opening wide to gather her daughter close. Her perfume wrapped Arianna in memories. She nestled for a few seconds longer than usual.

"Everything looks beautiful, Mom. What's the big event?"

"A luncheon for my book club."

Arianna leaned back. "I didn't know you were in a book club."

Her mother brushed the hair from Arianna's face and smiled. "We started it a few months ago. It's mostly an excuse to eat and gossip. We take turns hosting."

"And you're doing your own decorating? I'm impressed."

"That's part of the rules. I didn't iron the tablecloths myself," Paloma added in a whisper.

"A small cheat, Mom."

Paloma walked them to a table where she continued winding the leaf garland up the umbrella pole. Taller than her mother, Arianna took over as it reached the top then taped it there.

"You are looking demure today, *mija*," Paloma said, eyeing Arianna's jeans and white blouse.

"Good. That's the look I was going for."

"Are you undercover?"

"No." Well, sort of, she thought. "I'm meeting someone."

"Someone special?" her mother asked.

"Mike Vicente." Her heart pounded as she said the name.

"No." Paloma's face went ashen. She clasped her

daughter's hands. "You cannot. Arianna, you cannot. I forbid it."

Arianna squeezed back. "I have to know, Mom."

"Why? What good can come from this now, after all these years?"

"*My* good." *See how important this is to me, Mom.* "I need to find out what happened to my father."

"If they didn't know then, how can they know now?"

"A lot has changed. They're using DNA to solve old cases now."

Her mother shook her head.

"I've been having nightmares. Dad's trying to tell me something."

"Even if I believed in such things, why would he wait until now?"

Arianna willed her mother to understand. "Because something is different now. The truth is waiting. He wants me to find it."

"*Mija,* I am begging you to leave it alone."

"*Madre,* I can't." She forced the words out. "I can't rest until I know. I had hoped for your support, but I'll go ahead without it."

"I cannot endorse this. I cannot."

Arianna pulled her mother into a powerful hug. "I love you, Mom. I'll keep in touch."

After a few moments her mother hugged her back, her embrace fierce, as if she could stop her daughter from leaving. Finally she let go. *"Vaya con Dios, mija."*

"You, too, Mom." Arianna swallowed the lump in her throat and jogged back to her car. Her next conversation wouldn't be any easier.

From his parents' bedroom Joe could see the street, and every car that passed by. He didn't know what Arianna drove, but he imagined it was dark and sleek, like her. Something quiet and powerful. But maybe she would surprise him—again.

Her asking to meet his parents had almost left him speechless. After so many years as a detective he was accustomed to the routinely unpredictable nature of his work—things were often not as they seemed—but his relationships had been fairly predictable...if he didn't count Jane returning his engagement ring. That had caught him by surprise.

A dark blue BMW pulled up in front of the house. No surprise, after all. The trunk popped open, then she climbed out of the car, looking casual in jeans and a white top. Her shiny almost-black hair was down, the length just past her shoulders, which answered his question of last night. He missed the flamenco costume.

She shaded her eyes and looked at the house. He hurried down the stairs to meet her at her car, where she was unloading an ice chest.

"I hope you're hungry," she said, passing him the chest.

"Always." Joe noticed she wasn't making eye contact, unusual for her. The first time he met her he'd noticed how much eye contact she made, then noted it again last night. She started to walk past him, a grocery bag in hand. "Arianna."

"Hmm?"

Distracted wasn't the right word for her demeanor. She seemed nervous. Or anxious, maybe. "Hi. How are you?" he asked.

"Good, thanks. How are you?" She kept walking up the pathway to the house, a small, neat structure that his parents had owned since before he was born. "What a sweet house."

Joe tried to see it through her eyes. Freshly painted, the

yard well tended, mums in bloom. He'd put in long hours to get it looking good after a few years of neglect.

He followed Arianna into the house, also newly painted and spotless, although the furnishings were dated. "Kitchen's to your right," he said.

She walked into the room and set her bag on the counter. "Where are your parents?" she asked, looking around.

He put the ice chest next to the bag. "My mother passed away five months ago. My father just moved to a smaller place."

She stared speechlessly at him for several seconds then crossed her arms and looked at the floor. After what seemed like an hour she said, "I'm so sorry about your mother."

"Thank you. She put up a long, hard fight. Lung cancer," he added. "The house just sold. I'm doing an inventory of the contents so that I can figure out what to do with everything." What's going on? he wanted to ask. She was so subdued he didn't know what kind of conversation to have with her. He figured she would give him hell about implying there would be four for lunch. "Do you want to eat now?"

She roused herself enough to smile. "Sure. Anyone in the neighborhood you'd like to invite? There's enough here to feed ten, I think. Great bread. Marinated shrimp, barbecued chicken, several deli salads."

His stomach burned at the thought. Even bland food lit a fire. "I don't mind having leftovers." He took some plates from the cupboard and silverware from the drawer while she set out the containers.

"Do you want the bread heated?" she asked, holding up a loaf of something. If it wasn't sourdough or white sandwich bread he could only hazard a guess. This was brown, flat and oblong.

"Whatever you prefer." He figured she was a warm

bread kind of person. If she heated it, she meant to stay and have a conversation. If she didn't heat it, she planned a quick escape after the meal.

She moved to the stove and turned it on. He relaxed. Maybe he was reading something into her actions that wasn't there. She was normally confident and direct, but not today. Could she actually be nervous about being alone with him? Was that why she'd jumped at the chance of meeting him at his parents' house?

"I guess I should've told you my parents wouldn't be here," he said.

"That would've been nice." A brittle smile accompanied the razor-sharp tone.

He got it. She was mad. That he could handle.

"I didn't mean to mislead you, Arianna."

"You said you were going to be at your parents' house. You could easily have corrected my assumption that they would be here, but you didn't." Her eyes gave off sparks.

"I was too curious. Why would you want to meet my parents?" When she didn't answer, he moved to stand next to her. "What's going on?"

After a few seconds she faced him. "My father was murdered twenty-five years ago."

Like it was yesterday, he decided, seeing the pain in her eyes. "I'm sorry, Arianna. You must have been very young."

"Eight. Your father was the lead detective in charge of his case."

Surprise zapped him in the midsection, then he realized she must have known that fact before the party last night. He'd been set up. Used. "Is that why you wanted to meet him?"

"I want to know why he didn't find my father's killer."

Four

Arianna saw him retreat, not only physically by taking a step back, but his expression cooled, too.

"Some cases don't get solved. It's a sad fact of life," he said, crossing his arms. "So are you the reason I got an invitation to the party last night?"

She owed him the truth. "I saw a picture of you and Scott in his den last month when I had dinner there, and I asked about your relationship. Then I started having nightmares about my father." She brushed some crumbs off the counter with her hand, hoping he wouldn't see how much the dreams affected her. "For the first time since I was a little girl I got out the scrapbook I'd made after he died. I hadn't remembered the lead detective's name, Mike Vicente. It seemed too much of a coincidence, but I did some checking and found out he was your father."

"Then you asked Scott to invite me to the party so you could set me up."

She shook her head. "I wanted to talk to you. Away from your office."

"What made you think I wouldn't have talked to you? Met with you, away from the office? Did you figure you had to play the sex card to get my attention? I assure you, I'm not that base."

"The attraction was real and unplanned," she admitted. "Unfortunately."

"Unfortunately?"

"It complicated everything."

"You seemed to deal with that complication just fine. Nice dance, Arianna. Great kiss. I bought it."

His anger was justified, but it still stung. "I didn't know it was you by the waterfall. I had no idea." She couldn't tell if he believed her. His expression didn't change. "As for the kiss, I was as swept away as you were. The last thing I needed was—was…" She spread her hands wide, not able to come up with the right word.

"Chemistry?"

"Yes. I don't know if you've heard but I haven't exactly endeared myself to the LAPD through the years." Which was putting it mildly, she thought.

"I heard rumors," he said, then shrugged. "I asked around a little after we met."

"I have a lot of resentment."

"I gather that. At least now I know why."

She'd wondered. She'd thought maybe that was why he hadn't tried to contact her after they met last year. But that was before she knew he'd been engaged. "I figured you might have. But there's no denying we made some kind of connection when we met. I also figured if you got to know and like me, you would be more willing to do me a favor."

He shoved his hands in his back pockets. "What kind of favor?"

"I want to see my father's file. I had hoped you'd find a way to get it to me."

"All you have to do is request it."

"No. It's unsolved. I've been denied access."

"That makes no sense. If the case is twenty-five years old, what would it matter? Certainly you're entitled under the Freedom of Information Act."

"My relationship with the LAPD is bad enough already. Pushing legalities would only hurt me in the future when I need information for a case. All I want is to see the file. And find the killer," she added, the most important issue.

"Why do you think you could?"

"It's a hunch. I'm a good investigator, and I'm not bound by a cop's rules."

She could see him thinking it through.

"Was your father involved in a crime?" he asked.

"My father was a thirteen-year veteran of the Los Angeles Police Department. He died in the line of duty." A situation that still made her both angry and proud. He'd been her knight in shining armor—but he'd been taken from her.

Joe hardly missed a beat. He rested his palms on the counter and leaned toward her, his gaze locked with hers. "Then you know that my father and everyone else at the department did everything they could to find the killer and bring him to justice. Everything."

She didn't break eye contact. "And yet they didn't solve it. Tell me, Joe. If it was your father who had been murdered and justice hadn't been served, wouldn't you be doing everything in your power to find the killer?"

He was quiet long enough that she began to hope.

"I can't help you," he said at last, pushing away from the counter.

Hope died. "Why not?"

"A hot file like that—a cop whose line-of-duty death was never solved? That would require approval from some brass before I could pull it from Records. Plus, it would look like I was working, which I can't be, because I'm on vacation."

"When you get back from vacation, then."

"I'm off for four weeks starting today. If you can wait that long I'll give it a try."

She decided to press. "Would you let me talk to your father?"

"That's not possible." He picked up two of the food containers and carried them to the kitchen table.

"Why not?"

"I've given you my answer, Arianna. If things were different I would try to help you."

Her throat burned. He was her only chance of getting a look at the file, short of hiring a lawyer and making an issue out of it, which would totally destroy whatever small amount of credibility she had with the department. Not to mention that she needed the nightmares to end.

She looked blankly at all the food she'd brought. She couldn't stay there any longer.

Arianna extended her hand. "I'm sorry I bothered you."

He took her hand then didn't let go until she met his gaze. Sympathy brought out specks of gold in his green eyes, but he didn't try to stop her. She was grateful for that.

She kept her emotions in check as she pulled away from the curb. Now what? Where could she go? Not back to her mother's house. Not to her own apartment, either. Too quiet. To the office, then, where she spent most of her life, anyway.

She had to come up with plan B.

An hour later Joe tossed his inventory log onto the dining room table and headed to the backyard, in need of fresh air. He stalked the grounds, hunting for nonexistent weeds, then sat next to an orange tree and rested his back against the trunk. He plucked a blade of grass, then another. One more.

He didn't know why he'd expected anything different. Of course Arianna wasn't interested. He was a cop, LAPD at that—just like her father, a man who had died in the line of duty. And his own father hadn't found the killer.

That was just the beginning. Her income was probably three times his—or more. She had fit in at Scott's party, as sophisticated as the rest of his guests. Joe hadn't, which is why he'd discovered the waterfall in the first place. He had decided he'd made a mistake by going to the party and so had looked for a place to hang out until he could politely leave.

Then Arianna had appeared in the misty, mysterious place like a wish fulfilled, her spicy perfume alerting him to her presence, her sexy body jolting him back to life after a long sleep, her dark eyes entreating him to trust and hope. Was it all a game? She said it wasn't, that the attraction was real and unplanned and complicated. He would've believed her, believed she was honest, if she hadn't misled him last night. What was the truth?

He'd been lied to before, most recently by his own fiancée. He hadn't learned to play those games and didn't know how to spot the players.

Arianna hadn't shown herself to be any different. She'd walked out as soon as she learned he couldn't be of any use to her.

So much for trying to get back his life. And a date. It was too bad his interest had been piqued to the degree it had.

"Joe?"

He swung around. Arianna stepped through the side gate and into the yard.

"I didn't mean to just barge in, but I rang the bell several times. Your car was still out front, so I took a chance you were out here."

Damn, she was one sexy woman. Curvy, fluid, graceful and…competent.

"No problem," he said, standing to greet her. *Stay this time….*

"I apologize for walking out on you," she said.

He liked her directness and that she looked him in the eye. He even liked that she didn't offer an excuse. She was in search of the truth. He couldn't fault her for using whatever method it took to find that truth.

"Forget it," he said. "Are you hungry? I seem to have some extra food on hand."

After a moment she smiled. "I'm starving."

Keep it light, he told himself. "That's the real reason you came back."

"Absolutely. The only reason."

As they moved toward the house, he resisted resting his hand on her lower back as he had the night before, but her perfume whispered to him, urging him closer. He'd already danced with her. Kissed her. Held her against his body. He wanted to sweep her into his arms right now, but she wasn't a woman who could be rushed. He already knew that about her.

He also knew if he played his cards right, she might stay for dinner.

Arianna appreciated attractive men as much as the next woman—she just didn't trust them. There were exceptions. Her partners in her firm, Nate Caldwell and Sam Remington, were both attractive and trustworthy. And she sensed that Joe Vicente was a man she could trust. Maybe too much.

She let her gaze wander over him as he stored the left-overs in the otherwise empty refrigerator. He had the body type people called rangy—lean and loose-limbed. He moved slowly and spoke thoughtfully. A deliberate man, she decided. Someone who didn't make mistakes often, either in words or action. Important qualities in a detective. She wondered if his father was the same way.

She also wondered why Joe was protecting him.

Arianna hadn't realized her gaze was lingering on Joe's rear end until he turned around and caught her staring. In truth, although it was a very nice feature of his anatomy, she'd been lost in her own thoughts, not drooling. He couldn't have known that, however, and the last thing she wanted was to get involved, even just physically, with a man as wounded as he seemed to be.

Surprisingly, he didn't tease her. Instead he sat across from her at the kitchen table and said nothing, apparently letting her decide what would happen next.

She should probably go. She was keeping him from his task.

"Is this hard for you?" she asked instead. "Emptying your parents' house?"

"I grew up here. It's home."

"Do you *have* to sell it?"

"Yeah. Why'd you come back, Arianna?"

She'd been waiting for that question. He was a detective. He would want motive. "I don't know," she said honestly. "I started to drive to my office, but I got stuck in traffic, and I realized I didn't want to go there. I thought about how abrupt and rude I'd been, leaving like I did."

"You were disappointed."

"Greatly. But that's my problem, not yours. My mother

didn't want me to pursue it. Maybe I shouldn't.'' Making and keeping eye contact was ingrained in her. He matched her skill. She wasn't sure what he saw when he looked at her, but she couldn't shake how worn-out he looked. Protective instincts she'd never acknowledged before slammed into her, throwing her off balance. "Look, do you need help?"

His brows went up. "Help? With what?"

"With doing your inventory. Are you getting things ready for a garage sale?"

"I'm taking what I want to keep and deciding what to donate and what to toss."

She couldn't figure him out. Last night he'd taken charge, his good-night kiss even more memorable because of his complete command of the moment. Today he seemed to be holding back, waiting for her to make a move.

Fine. Good. She didn't want him to pursue her, anyway, right? She didn't need that kind of complication. She'd been careful not to become involved with a cop, not even once. She could resist him.

"Are you offering to help?" Joe asked.

"I'd be happy to." The words spilled out unchecked. To cover her astonishment, she pushed away from the table and glanced at her watch. "I have to be home by six o'clock."

"Four hours is more than enough time," he said, also standing.

"I have a date," she added, almost wincing at the defensive tone in her voice.

"I see."

She heard the smile in his voice. She hadn't been this rattled since...she couldn't remember when. A woman in her profession couldn't afford to be.

But then, this wasn't business.

* * *

In the attic, Joe watched Arianna wrap a framed photograph in newspaper and pack it carefully in a box, as if it were her treasure, not his. What he'd heard about her when he'd inquired around the department last year was that she was tough, smart and unsentimental, facts he'd observed for himself when she'd provided him with information on the Wells case last year. Their involvement had been brief and businesslike, with a hint of male/female awareness making the meeting interesting. But he'd also been engaged to Jane. In all the complications of his life since then he'd forgotten about Arianna.

He wondered now how he could have. Anyone who thought her unsentimental hadn't seen her expression when she ordered him to go do something else so she could pack his mother's clothes. She'd even shut the closet door before he returned so he wouldn't see the empty space. He would remember her kindness.

Joe glanced at his watch. She would have to leave soon. For her date. He didn't know why he'd assumed she wasn't involved with anyone. Maybe because last night she'd come to the party alone, and danced with him, and kissed him back.

But last night she'd come to the party for a purpose—to meet him. She wouldn't have brought a boyfriend along. It would've been business to her.

She was a damned challenging woman. And he liked predictable.

"What's in those boxes?" she asked, pointing to the last ones, tucked under the eaves.

He closed the lid on the trunk he'd been rummaging through, deciding he needed to keep everything in it. Relics of past generations.

Joe dragged the four unmarked boxes into the center of the room and opened one. His heart began to pound. He opened the second box, then he looked at Arianna. "Files," he said. "My father's old case files."

Her eyes widened. She sat up straight but said nothing. Was she waiting for him to offer her the files? Of course she was.

"You're welcome to stay and look through them," he said.

"Don't you need to ask your father's permission?"

He hesitated, then shook his head.

She pulled her cell phone out of her back pocket and dialed. "Jordan, hi, it's me. Look, I'm sorry to do this but I need to cancel our plans for tonight…. No, not work, but something important. Can I call you tomorrow?… Terrific. Thanks. Bye."

Joe could measure her excitement not by her voice or her face, both of which she controlled remarkably, but by her hands, which shook. He shoved one box toward her.

She said nothing. She didn't have to.

He worried they were opening a Pandora's box.

The sounds of manila folders and paper being shuffled replaced conversation. Tension filled the air like smoke from a smoldering fire, thick and acrid, making it hard to breathe. Joe admitted to himself that he was as anxious as Arianna to find the file, to know what happened. How she had become that important to him that fast wasn't something he wanted to examine very closely, but he felt her anticipation—and her dread—as strongly as if it were coming from inside him.

"They're not in any order," she said after flipping through the first few files. "They should be in order, either alphabetically or by date, wouldn't you think?"

"Yeah." The neatly typed labels mocked them. They should have represented organization, the ability to put your hands on the right folder any time. Instead, twenty years of files were tossed haphazardly into boxes as if one had no more relevance than another.

Or as if someone had searched through them, not returning them to their proper order.

"I found it," Arianna said, but without excitement or urgency. Silence roared through the tiny attic space. She held up a file, opened it. "Empty."

Empty—worse than the potential Pandora's box. No truths revealed. No illusions shattered. No answers for a daughter who desperately needed them—and maybe a son, too, who wanted to know how a cop killing could go unsolved.

Five

Arianna resisted the urge to scream. Instead she drew on her martial arts and yoga training by controlling her breathing and visualizing the sun setting into the ocean.

"The files are jumbled," Joe said into her growing calm. "Maybe the papers got mixed with another file."

"Maybe."

"Let's take the boxes to the dining room." He scooped up one box and hauled it down the pull-down attic stairs then shouted back up to her. "Pass me the others, okay?"

That got her moving. Fifteen minutes later they were settled in the dining room, the old maple table stacked with folders.

She examined her father's file. The tag was typed with his name, Mateo Alvarado, the date of his murder and another series of numbers. She thumbed through some other folders. "Look at this," she said, pointing. "My father's tag has an extra set of numbers typed on it. As far as I can tell, it's the only one.''

Joe made a quick check of the stack nearest him. ''None of these, either. Just name and date.''

Arianna puzzled over it for a few seconds then opened the empty folder again. Closed it. Opened it. ''Wouldn't a homicide investigation produce a lot of paperwork?''

''Sure. Crime-scene analyses, witness reports, forensics. In the case of a cop within his own department? There would be extra interviews and copies of media coverage. Why?''

''Look at the folder. The crease is still sharp-edged, as if nothing was ever placed in there at all.''

He met her gaze. ''I don't know what that could mean.''

''It's odd, though, right?''

''Yeah. Even for an open-and-shut-case, it would be odd.'' He turned his attention back to the folders in front of him. ''So we'll go through all the files page by page. If it's there, we'll find it.''

''Why wouldn't it be there?'' she asked, dragging a file closer.

''I don't know. Maybe my dad started as the primary but the case was given to someone else and he turned over his notes.''

''Can you call and ask him?''

''No.''

His casual tone irritated her, but she knew she couldn't push him. She did wonder what the big deal was.

''I heard a rumor you were in the army,'' he said.

Arianna allowed the change of subject. ''For eight years.''

''You must've joined right out of high school.''

''A week after graduation.''

''Why?''

Why? She wondered how to explain it so that he understood. "Do you know who my stepfather is?"

"No idea."

"Estebán Clemente."

That got his attention. "The movie guy?" He frowned. "You weren't…escaping him, were you?"

His reaction took her by surprise. "Not in the way you mean. He is a loving man, although strict. Very strict."

She saw his shoulders loosen. "How did your mother meet him?"

"After my father died, she started taking me to auditions for television commercials, something I'd wanted to do forever but which my father had forbidden. I landed a few spots and some print ads, as well, enough to keep me busy."

"Weren't you only eight years old?"

She nodded.

"Was it something *you* wanted or your mother wanted?"

"I wanted it. I did well, too. Then when I had just turned twelve I auditioned for a movie that Estebán was producing. I was cast in a small part. Maria Sanchez, rebel teenager," she said, remembering the role fondly. "Estebán came to the set on a day I was working. He met my mother, and it was instant fireworks." She put a file aside and grabbed another. "A couple of months later they were married, and the first thing he did was lay down the law. No more auditions. He said it was a bad business for children and he wouldn't allow it. My mother supported him, of course. I was angry for years. Years."

She caught Joe smiling. "What?"

"Just picturing you angry. Spitfire."

"I hated him. I made his life miserable."

"What did he do?"

"Kept the reins tight. Tolerated me. He said he didn't

care if I liked him or not, that his job was to provide for me and care for me, and he was damned well going to do his job, even if I hated him the rest of my life."

"I like him."

"You would."

Joe nodded sagely. "So, all this caring and providing was so hard to take that you enlisted. I see. Makes sense."

She gave him a cool look. "Do you want to hear this story or not?"

"I do."

"Then don't be sarcastic." She turned the cover on another file. "Estebán expected me to go to college."

"He should've been shot."

She clamped her mouth shut, mostly against a smile, because now that she was grown up, she did see how juvenile she'd been at the time. "That's it. I'm not telling you the rest."

Joe laughed quietly. "What did *you* want to do?"

"I wanted to tramp across Europe for a year first. You know, experience life."

"That doesn't sound so bad."

"Exactly! Where were you when I needed you?"

A couple of beats passed. "Patrolling the streets of Los Angeles, keeping you safe from harm," he said finally. "I take it he refused to support your goal."

"Not only would he not support me—he wouldn't even help. I would've had money to do it on my own if he'd let me keep working as an actor. But, no. It was his way or the highway. I chose the highway."

"But, the army? Why? You were eighteen. You didn't have to do what he said anymore."

"Because I had no way of supporting myself other than minimum wage jobs. I figured it was the best opportunity for me. And I was right. I even reenlisted when I had the chance. It was a great experience.''

''You know, Arianna, I can't quite picture you taking orders.''

''I'm not saying I could've done it forever, but it was a good learning experience. I had been sheltered at home. In the army I learned to stand on my own two feet. I almost died once.'' She stopped. She rarely discussed it. ''I appreciate life because of it,'' she finished, then was quiet a moment before asking, ''How about you? Why'd you become a cop?''

''The obvious answer is because of my dad.''

''But that's not why?''

''It's part of it.'' He put a folder aside, picked up another but didn't open it. ''I thought I could make a difference.''

''Have you?''

''Sometimes. And sometimes it's just routine and frustrating and aggravating. How did you almost die?''

She knew he wasn't going to let her off the hook. ''Ironically, on a peace-keeping mission. A bomb blast that demolished our barracks. My partners, Nate and Sam, and I were trapped together for two days.''

''Were you hurt?''

''Bumps and bruises. Sam broke his leg.''

Joe sat back in his chair, questioning without saying anything.

''While we were stuck in the rubble waiting for help,'' she continued, ''we came up with a plan to start our own security and investigation firm. We spent all our awake time figuring it out. I knew Estebán would line us up with contacts at first. And I knew once we got a chance to prove ourselves, we would succeed.'' She paid attention to the folder in front of her again. ''I don't have scars from the experience. How about you?''

"Scars? Not from the job."

His expression changed instantly, as if he realized he'd said too much. He picked up another folder even though he hadn't opened the one in front of him. When he realized what he'd done, he stood. "I'm going to get a beer. Want one?"

"Sure." She wondered if his scars were from the break-up with his fiancée.

They sat at the table until her shoulders and back ached. The emotional upheaval exhausted her even more. As the stack of files dwindled so did her hope. The papers hadn't been misfiled. They were gone. Or nonexistent.

She tossed the last folder onto the stack and waited until he was done and did the same. "His was the only empty folder," she said.

He dragged his hands down his face. "Yeah."

"I don't understand, Joe."

"I don't either."

She waited for him to offer to ask his father. He didn't.

Arianna looked at her watch and stood, worn out, irritated and disappointed. She dug her keys out of her pocket. "I should get going."

He was slower to stand, but he finally walked with her to the front door. A kind of force field stopped her there. She didn't know what else to call it, but something made her hesitate rather than open the door.

"When you get back from your vacation you'll try to get the file from Records?" she asked, facing him.

"No promises."

She nodded. Still she didn't move. Couldn't move. She wanted…something. Frustration over not finding her father's folder swirled inside her, gathering impotent speed. She wasn't used to feeling helpless, but she felt helpless now. And alone.

"Well," she said, not looking at him but at the doorknob instead.

"Arianna." He said her name with such sympathy.

She couldn't form any words.

With a soft murmur of comfort he slipped his arms around her and tucked her close. Her eyes stung. Men didn't usually hold her—just hold her—probably because she didn't let them, preferring to stay in charge and in control. But she not only let Joe hold her, she moved closer, relaxing into him. When they were body to body his embrace tightened. She squeezed back. His scent had her nuzzling his neck. Their thighs rubbed together. Everywhere in between he felt wonderful. Long and lean and strong and sexy.

She lost track of time—long enough for her thoughts to shift from pleasure to awareness. There was a power about him that drew her even as his touch was tender, his hand stroking her hair, soothing, and his breath dusting her cheek, creating chills of anticipation. She yearned for him in a way she couldn't remember yearning before. This kiss was going to be one for the record books.

He leaned away, looked into her eyes, brushed her hair back, then left his hands along her face. He held her gaze for long seconds. Then he kissed her forehead. She closed her eyes and waited for his lips to touch her cheek, her other cheek, her lips....

"I'm sorry we didn't find what you wanted," he said against her hair.

His sympathy caught her off guard. "Me, too," she said, trying to focus on the shift of mood. "Thank you for trying, though."

She tipped her head back and looked at him. She already knew how his lips were a perfect combination of hard and soft, tender and tempting.

"I guess your friend Jordan is used to you canceling dates," he said, taking a step back, releasing her. "You must get emergency calls all the time."

Icy surprise replaced the heat of the moment, but she'd be damned if she would let him see how stunned she was.

He had an interesting way of interrogating. Relax the suspect then go in for the kill. "A lot of our work is urgent and time-sensitive," she said, all business. "And we're in demand outside L.A. a lot more these days. In fact, we're getting so many assignments in San Francisco that we're thinking about opening a branch office there."

He crossed his arms. "Would you move?"

"No. Sam might consider it, at least until the office is well established. His wife has a home there."

"That's right. He married the senator."

"They're on their honeymoon. To answer your first question, though, yes, Jordan is used to me canceling. She's fine with it, though."

His hesitation was short but telling. "She?"

"We've been friends since high school. Jordan Maria Morelli."

His mouth twitched. "Did you enjoy that, Arianna?"

"What?"

"Letting me think you had a date."

"I did have a date. With my friend, Jordan. We were going to see the Jackie Chan marathon."

He laughed. "Figures. You're probably a martial arts expert."

"*Tae kwon do.*"

"Why that one?"

"Because kicks are generally more powerful than punches, which gives a woman an advantage. But the training is about how to avoid putting yourself in dangerous or uncontrolled situations. If I find myself in a position where

I have to fight in order to protect myself, it's probably because I made an error in judgment. I'm especially alert if I'm doing personal protection, particularly celebrities. Anything can happen.''

"You do a threat assessment."

"Constantly." She'd stalled as long as possible. At some point she had to leave—and come to terms with her disappointment, not only because she'd struck out on finding her father's file but because Joe hadn't kissed her.

She acknowledged that her ego was stung, but after a second she met his innocent gaze and smiled. When he'd made the decision not to kiss her, it was the same as tossing down the gauntlet, challenging her. And she couldn't pick it up without seeing him again.

A fact he knew.

"Score one for you," she said, not backing down.

His brows lifted. "Excuse me?"

"You know what I'm talking about." She could see from his expression that he was completely aware of his effect on her.

He moved in on her just a little. "Are we in a competition, Arianna?"

"We're in something. I don't know exactly what."

He grinned. "Neither do I, but can I get a rematch?"

She came so close to telling him to name the time and place. So close. But he was a cop, one with a too-close-for-comfort connection to the man she'd hated all these years. The man who hadn't found justice for her father. She couldn't forget that. She wasn't vindictive—the sins of the father would not be laid upon the son—but the connection was too strange.

Even though he tempted her beyond anyone in her memory. Even though his unspoken challenge started a fire in her, one she wasn't sure could be extinguished easily.

She jangled her keys. "Good night, Detective."

"You have my number." He dragged a finger down her cheek, lifted her hair over her ear to run his fingertip around the shell then leaned close to say, "I'm in Olympic form, by the way."

He stole her breath with his sexy tone of voice. "For what event?" she asked.

"A marathon." He kissed that tender spot right below her ear.

She closed her eyes. "Twenty-six miles?"

"Twenty-six hours."

Arianna's imagination went wild with possibilities. "Athletes are supposed to abstain before big events."

His laugh was low and husky. "I have been abstaining. The marathon would be the big event."

"Oh."

He pulled his head back enough to make eye contact. "I'm good for a sprint, but mostly, Arianna, I'm a long-distance runner."

"Good to know." She walked away wondering if she'd just made the biggest mistake of her life.

Six

More than a week later Arianna sat behind her desk and studied her partners as they discussed active cases over a late lunch, their first opportunity since Sam had returned from his honeymoon. The two men couldn't be more opposite, she thought, although at their cores, they were similar—intelligent, reliable, trustworthy and loyal. But Nate Caldwell was blond, easygoing and social, the most publicly visible of the partners, and Sam Remington was dark, serious and a very private man—at least until he'd married U.S. Senator Dana Sterling two weeks ago. Arianna fell somewhere in the middle, both a public and private person. She was also the managing partner in ARC Security & Investigations because she hated paperwork the least of the three of them.

Today she was surrounded by paperwork—current case files, billings, expense account statements, and résumés. They needed to hire at least two more investigators, bringing their total to fourteen. More support staff would soon follow.

"We need to get serious about San Francisco," she said, as Nate and Sam ended their discussion. "We've got to get someone local, ASAP." Arianna looked at Sam, questioning silently, as did Nate.

"I could move there for now," Sam said. "But once Dana's term is up, we plan to live here. She's probably going to teach at UCLA."

"Any ideas on who we could get?" Arianna asked.

"One." Sam leaned back. "I only know him as Doc. Met him when we were working the Douglas Walker case a couple years back. We were hired by different family members but to do the same job—find out who was embezzling from the family business. Our paths crossed. We worked together."

"Doc? All we need is Happy and Grumpy and we've got ourselves a branch office," Nate said with a grin. "Hey, it's San Francisco. We can probably even find a receptionist named Snow."

"Obviously we're not putting you in charge of the hiring," Arianna said dryly. "What impressed you about him, Sam?"

"He didn't get territorial over his findings, which is rare, as you know. Plus he could make himself invisible."

"You're good at that."

"He's better. He keeps to the shadows even more. And he's got computer skills beyond mine."

"Hard to believe. You gonna finish that?" Nate asked, pointing to Arianna's unfinished turkey sandwich, grabbing it when she shook her head. "Problem is, loners don't like to work for someone else. He'll demand his own terms."

"The good ones always do," Arianna said. "But, Sam, if he's that mysterious, how do we get in touch with him?"

"I can track him down."

Arianna had no doubt about that. She tapped her pen on her desktop. "He sounds like someone who picks and chooses his clients. Would he work for a firm where he'd be assigned cases?"

"I don't know, but you asked for names, and he's the only one I can think of who's good enough to maintain our reputation. That's critical. If you both agree, I'll check him out."

Nate nodded.

Arianna's intercom beeped. She hit the speaker button. "Yes, Julie?"

"There's a Joe Vicente on line two."

Arianna's heart thumped. Sam and Nate seemed to come to attention. She tried not to react. "Would you tell him I'll call him back shortly, please."

"He says it's urgent."

Urgent. Her stomach lurched. "Okay. Thanks. I'll take it." Before she pushed the line-two button she looked at Nate and Sam. "If that's all…?"

"Joe Vicente," Nate said thoughtfully. "Wasn't he the LAPD cop in charge of Alexis Wells's case last year? Sam told me about him, I think. As I recall Sam said you were oozing pheromones all around him, Ar."

"Go away, Nate."

"You're blushing," Nate said, his surprise wiping out the previous teasing tone. "When did this become a thing?"

"It's not a thing. He's helping me with something. Go away."

Nate stuffed the last of the sandwich in his mouth and left the room with a backward wave.

Sam trapped her with his gaze. "You okay, Ar?"

"Yes."

He watched her for a few more seconds then he, too, left, shutting the door behind him without being asked.

Over the past week Arianna had done her best to ignore Joe's existence. Wasted energy. If anything, her reaction was stronger. She couldn't remember her mouth going dry over a man before.

She drew a ragged breath then picked up the phone. "Good morning, Detective."

"That won't work, you know."

She clenched the receiver. He sounded good—warm and playful. "What won't?"

"Calling me Detective. Trying to keep this all business between us."

"It is business."

"No. It isn't. Except at the moment."

She sat up. "You found the file."

"Yes."

"Where?"

"I'll tell you when I see you."

"Will you bring it here to the office?"

A beat passed. "No."

She bit back her impatience. "Do you want me to come to your parents' house?"

"My house. I'll give you the address."

She wrote it down, as well as the directions. "I'll be there as soon as I can."

"Keep it at the speed limit."

She smiled. "Yes, sir. Joe?"

"What?"

"Are the answers there?"

"You can read the file, Arianna. I'll be waiting for you." He hung up.

She took a minute to settle herself. Finally she would have the facts. She could find the truth. Then the nightmares would end.

Joe leaned against his front porch pillar, waiting for Arianna. He wished he could invite her to sit and talk for a while first, but reading the file would be her priority. He couldn't blame her for that.

It had been hard not calling her all week, but especially over the weekend, when days always seem longer alone. Insomnia still kept him company at night, and his stomach burned like the devil had sold it a franchise, but added to the mix now was Arianna. Smart, sexy Arianna.

He saw her car approach. He wondered where she lived. In some contemporary house with a pool, probably. In his neighborhood of mostly eighty-year-old bungalows, people were buying and renovating houses with an eye for tradition. He liked watching the transformations, especially since he'd invested a lot of time and money redoing his house five years ago when he moved in.

Arianna came up the front walk, her stride leisurely but her body tense. She wore a deep-green jacket and skirt, which landed a few inches above her knees. High heels added to her height. Her blouse was white and simple, a deep V giving a hint of cleavage, where a simple gold pendant nestled. He'd bet she didn't own anything with frills or flowers. The tailored look suited her, made her seem even more feminine.

She pulled off her sunglasses as she stopped beside him on the porch. Her hair shimmered in the sunlight. Her eyes glittered. Tension bracketed her mouth. She said nothing. He understood that she was too emotional to speak.

He rested a hand on her shoulder. "I took down a painting in my parents' bedroom. It had been there for as long as I can remember," he said, giving her the details. "I found a safe behind it. I had no idea what the combination was. I searched through everything. Then I remembered the numbers on your father's file label. The only file with that kind of number. I tried it. It worked. Inside was his paper-work.''

''Anything else?''

''My mother's pearls, handed down from mother to daughter for five generations. A Smith & Wesson .38 revolver. It may be a police issue, but it may not. I'll have to check what was issued in the seventies. Dad had a gun safe. I don't know why that particular weapon was in his personal safe. I hesitate to make assumptions. However, the serial number was filed off the weapon.''

Her brows furrowed. ''You think—''

''I don't know what to think. I don't want to guess.'' He pushed away from the pillar. ''Everything's stacked on my desk in my office.''

He led the way, wondering what she thought of his house that he'd painstakingly gutted and restored in true bunga-low style. The furnishings weren't overly masculine. He'd tried to create a house he could bring a wife to, a home for children to grow and laugh and come home to visit when they were grown. He'd thought Jane would be that wife. She'd led him to believe it. Then she'd walked away when the going got tough.

It was better to have learned her character before the wedding, but that was small consolation for heartache— and for being so wrong about someone.

''Do you want something to drink?'' he asked Arianna, knowing her answer would be no.

''No, thank you.''

''Have a seat.''

She sat behind his desk and stared at the stack in front of her. ''It's a big file.''

"He was a murdered cop."

She spread her hands over the pile. "Can't you just tell me what's here?"

"No." He knew she needed to see it, to read it for herself. There were newspaper clippings. Crime-scene photos. A videotape of it, too, and of the funeral. Arianna, at age eight, had been stoic even then—until her father's coffin was lowered into the ground. Watching it had wrenched his heart and chilled his soul.

He took a seat across from her, watched as she slowly pored through the paperwork, including his father's notebook. Joe had taken the crime-scene photos and tape out of the packet and put them in a drawer. She didn't need to see those.

"I don't understand," she said after a long time. "I mean that literally. I can't understand his notes. Can you?"

"Very little of it."

"It's so cryptic. Like some kind of shorthand. Or code."

"Yeah."

She pushed herself up, the force knocking her chair over. She ignored it.

"We're no closer now than we were without the file," she said, exasperation in her voice. "It's gibberish."

"It has to mean something."

She paced. Along the way she straightened pictures on the wall, and the plaques for honors he'd won in high school as varsity quarterback. Trophies filled a bookcase, not only for football, but baseball, too.

She stopped at last and turned to look at him. He knew what she would say before she said it.

"I have to talk to your father."

Seven

Arianna waited for his answer. She heard a clock ticking and looked for it, spotting it on a table beside a big leather chair. She focused on the clock—on time. Time passing…running out…gone by.

Time flies. Drags. Stands still.

Time waits for no man.

Time heals all wounds.

Long time no see.

"Okay," Joe said, resignation in his voice. "Okay."

Her tension let go all at once and light-headedness took over. She reached blindly for something to hold on to. She felt his hand grip hers. His arm slid around her waist.

"Sit down," he said, moving her to the leather chair, kneeling beside her. "Breathe slowly."

She prided herself on her ability to control her emotions, but the tidal wave crashing down on her had her floundering for her footing. "I'm all right," she said, maybe more to herself than to him.

"Just relax. Do you want some water?"

She shook her head. "I just want to see your father."

He stood, hesitated. "I'll back my car out of the garage. Stay here for a minute."

"I'm fine," she insisted. "I'll go with you."

"Suit yourself."

Arianna gathered the materials and slid them into a canvas bag lying on the desk. In the early evening duskiness they walked in silence to the garage, then drove without speaking a few miles before pulling up in front of a well-maintained two-story Spanish-style house. Small yucca trees and shiny-leafed bird-of-paradise plants helped soften the lines of the house. The lawn was neat and trimmed.

And bars covered the windows.

She climbed out of the car and walked beside Joe to the front door. He didn't knock but let himself in with a key. Their footsteps echoed in the Spanish-tile entry hall. The house seemed deserted.

"Wait here," he said, then left her standing alone by the front door.

She pulled a small mirror out of her pocket, combed her hair with her fingers, and swiped her hands across her cheeks to bring color to her face. She tugged on her jacket, wishing she'd worn pants today instead of a skirt.

"Arianna." His voice surprised her. She hadn't heard him return. "Come this way."

He led her down a hall and into a room, letting her precede him. The room was well lit. She spotted a man seated in a chair by a window. He smiled when they entered. He looked so much like Joe that Arianna stopped in her tracks. Older, yes, but the same full head of hair, only gray. The

same green eyes and strong jaw. He wore a blue jogging
suit. And slippers.

"Hi, Dad. It's Joe," Joe said, passing by Arianna to go
to his father and giving him a kiss on the cheek.

A yellow Lab sat up and wagged its tail, then laid its
head in Mr. Vicente's lap and got a pat on the head. An
old dog, Arianna decided, but one who loved its master.

"Hi, Chief. Hey, buddy," Joe said, scratching the dog
behind the ears.

Mr. Vicente continued to smile but there was no recog-
nition in his eyes. Alzheimer's, she realized. She would find
no answers here.

"This is my friend, Arianna," Joe said.

"Hello," Mr. Vicente said.

Reaction tumbled through her. Anger and hurt that Joe
hadn't told her what was wrong with his father so that she
would've been prepared. Frustration that once again she
had hit a brick wall in her investigation of her father's
death. Sadness for Joe, too. He'd lost his mother to lung
cancer, and now he dealt with this.

She moved closer to Mr. Vicente and bent toward him.
"Hello. I'm happy to meet you." Chief nudged her with
his wet nose.

Mr. Vicente looked at Joe, who crouched beside him,
taking his father's hand in his. "Mrs. Winters said you went
to the park today and saw the squirrels."

He perked up. "Squirrels. They like nuts." He slipped
a frail hand into his jacket pocket and fished around.
"Nope. No nuts. Squirrels. They like nuts."

"I'll bring some for your next trip to the park."

"Okay. Okay, Tommy."

Arianna wondered who Tommy was. Joe shut his eyes
for a moment before he answered.

"Okay, Dad."

"Can you get some nuts?"

"Yes, Dad. I'll bring some next time."

His father stroked Joe's hair, his smile soft, his eyes tender. A memory slammed into Arianna of Mike Vicente years ago, coming to her house after the murder. She'd forgotten. She'd forgotten the soft-spoken man who'd stood by in silence as her mother screamed at him, and Arianna got caught up in the high tension. Protective of her mother, she'd also been drawn to the comfort he'd seemed to offer. He'd asked if there was anything he could do for her, and she'd wanted to fling herself into his arms and stay there. Instead she'd kicked his shins and yelled at him to leave them alone.

All that came rushing back to Arianna in a flash, a memory embedded all these years.

"I remember you," Arianna said now, her throat burning. "You came to my house. You were kind. Thank you for your kindness."

He smiled as if he remembered what she was talking about, but his eyes were vacant. "You're welcome."

She glanced at Joe, saw the question in his eyes through the blur in her own.

"Can I get you anything, Dad?" he asked.

"No. No. I'm fine."

"Okay. I'll see you tomorrow." He kissed his father's forehead as he stood.

Arianna put out her hand. "Goodbye, Mr. Vicente. I'm happy to have seen you again."

He looked at her hand for a few seconds, then put out his left hand and squeezed hers. His skin felt papery, his bones fragile. His gaze seemed to sharpen, though.

"You look like your mother," he said as she started to move away.

Startled, Arianna glanced at Joe, who looked intently at his father. "I do?" she asked.

"She was beautiful, your mother."

He remembered her mother? "Thank you. I think so, too."

"I loved her, you know."

Oh. Not her mother, then. Someone else. Someone special.

Joe took her by the arm and pulled her along with him. "Bye, Dad."

"Goodbye, Tommy."

She didn't say anything until they were in the car. He put the key in the ignition but didn't start the engine, apparently knowing she needed to talk first.

"You could've told me," she said.

"You had to see for yourself. You wouldn't have believed me."

Maybe he was right. She would've believed, but not as much as seeing proof. "How long has he been that way?"

"He was diagnosed three years ago, but the illness progressed slowly. Mom took care of him at home even while she was having chemo. Toward the end she allowed home-care nurses during the day. I stayed at the house at night. Then after Mom died, I took over his care, until I couldn't anymore." He looked out the windshield. "I just couldn't."

"So, you're selling the house to pay for his care?"

"It's expensive. Obscenely expensive. But I want him in a good facility, well taken care of. He deserves that. He's seventy-one. He could live for—for a while yet."

"And when the money from the sale of the house is gone?"

"I'll sell mine."

Three words that said so much about the man. She swallowed. "Who is Tommy?"

"His brother, who died when he was about my age."

"Does he ever recognize you?"

"Hardly at all anymore. I come every day to see him, and every day I hope. He calls Chief by the name of the dog we had when I was a teenager, Sarge." He blew out a breath. "I thought maybe he really did recognize you for a minute, but he was obviously talking about someone else." He angled toward her more. "You honestly remember him coming to your house?"

She nodded. "He came several times, actually. I'd totally forgotten. My mother was out of her mind with grief. She treated him very badly, worse every time he came. He just stood there and took it. In retrospect I see that she must have been so frustrated and angry that the killer hadn't been found, but then all I knew was that your father seemed to be hurting my mother by whatever he said to her. To look at her now, you would never believe her capable of such behavior. Nothing seems to throw her."

"Like mother, like daughter." He started the engine and pulled away.

She wasn't sure if he was insulting or complimenting her. "It's a handy skill as an investigator."

"I'm sure."

She couldn't get a handle on his mood. "Thank you for sharing your father with me. I know it was hard, given his condition."

He sent a quick, searching gaze toward her. "I'm not embarrassed by him."

"I didn't mean—"

"I just didn't want you to subject him to a bunch of questions I knew he couldn't answer."

"You're protective. I understand. He's very sweet."

"Fortunately, he's docile. Some Alzheimer's patients become hostile and uncontrollable. He could still reach that state. Anytime, actually."

"Does he talk about your mother?"

"Yes. The thing about Alzheimer's is that the person's life is being run backward, like a videotape winding in reverse. He regresses. That's why he's calling me Tommy at the moment—because I'm the same age as Tommy was when he died. If I would show him a picture of Mom right before she died, he wouldn't recognize her. But one taken when she was about fifty, he would know." His voice softened. "I found him crying one day. He'd realized Mom was gone, and then the moment was over and he went back into his world."

Arianna wondered about Joe. It sounded like he'd been the caregiver for a long time. His fiancée had apparently been out of the picture for a while. Who made his life easier so that he could bear his own load?

She studied him as he drove. He was a homebody, a family man, even though he didn't have much family at the moment. He had a nice home in a real neighborhood. He loved and cared about his parents. He'd loved a woman enough to ask her to marry him. Something had gone terribly wrong there.

In general, cops often made bad spouses. Out of necessity they buried their feelings because they saw so much horror in the world that they didn't want to share with a partner, but that often meant they buried *all* emotion. Had his fiancée not been able to draw him out? Had she felt left out because he wouldn't share? Had he not trusted her enough to share his burdens?

Arianna's own track record definitely didn't make her an expert in how to make a relationship work. Her career had come first since the day she graduated from high school.

Nothing had happened to change that. Like her father, she was devoted to her job. Success mattered to her. Respect mattered even more.

"Would you like to go out to dinner?" Joe asked as he stopped short of pulling into his garage. "Or we could order takeout."

"I'm not hungry. But thanks." She clutched the bag with the file to her chest. She wanted to go home and start trying to make sense of his father's notes.

"Arianna."

"Hmm?"

He tapped the packet. "The videotape in there is of your father's funeral."

She loosened her hold and looked down. "Okay."

"I don't want you to watch it alone, not the first time, anyway."

"Why not? What's on it?" A bit of panic set in. What could be there that he didn't think she should see?

"Your memories of the funeral are one thing. Actually seeing it is another. I just don't think you should watch it by yourself."

"Fine. Can we watch it now?"

"Yes."

Several minutes later they were seated in his living room, a comfortable room that combined simply designed wood pieces with cozy upholstered ones.

"Remember this is a police video," he said. "They were taping in hopes of seeing someone who didn't belong, who might have been the shooter. So there are a lot of crowd scenes. It starts at the church, then it moves to the cemetery."

"All right." She wondered if that was the voice he might use to talk someone down off a ledge. Calm, factual and soothing all at the same time.

He sat about a foot away from her on the sofa then aimed the remote at the television and started the video. Suddenly she wished she was alone, so that she could just let herself react to whatever it was she was about to see, without Joe witnessing it. He'd already seen her more vulnerable than anyone since she, Nate and Sam had thought they might die together and had shared their deepest secrets and dreams. She'd always figured little in life could be worse than that.

She hadn't counted on being vulnerable to a man who appealed to her on so many levels—emotionally, intellectually and physically. She'd been right in her impression of him on Halloween night. He was a kindred spirit—battle weary and driven by demons, only his were more visible than hers. Hers had been buried for twenty-five years and had only recently resurfaced. She didn't know how her plunge into her past was going to turn out. She just knew she had to deal with it, whatever it turned up.

Arianna didn't comment as she watched the tape, which panned the crowds again and again. The film was grainy, the sound masked by static and crowd noise, but she was mesmerized by it all once the funeral service started. She would watch it again with the volume turned up so she could try to understand the tributes to her father. When the ceremony ended, the chief of police, who had delivered one of the eulogies, escorted her mother and her up the aisle.

She leaned forward, her eyes on the image of her mother at age thirty-three, the same age as Arianna now. Dressed in black, Paloma looked haggard from exhaustion and grief. Arianna realized she hadn't seen her mother wear black since that day. Instead she chose vibrant colors, not owning even one basic black dress, unusual in her social circle.

Joe shifted beside her as the film switched to the grave-side service. She couldn't hear the words spoken by the chaplain but heard a gun salute, which made her jump. Then the coffin was lowered into the ground and she saw herself scream and call for him again and again as her mother tried to hold her back and soothe her while others looked on helplessly. The tape turned even grainier, then she realized it wasn't the tape but that she was crying. She hadn't remembered the scene at the gravesite. She wished she hadn't seen it, been reminded of it. She had called "Daddy" until her voice went hoarse from the salty tears coating her throat.

She felt Joe's hand come to rest on her shoulder, and she sloughed it off. He held a box of tissues toward her. She couldn't look at him. Couldn't speak. She grabbed several tissues, swiped them under her eyes, and tried not to let the tears turn to sobs, even as they welled up in her chest, pressing painfully, seeking release.

The tape ended. She didn't move.

"I'm sorry," he said.

"It was a long time ago."

"Arianna—"

"Don't, okay? Just don't." She stood. Looked around. Now what? She needed to go home. She couldn't drive herself yet, that much she knew. "I need to find out who killed him," she said.

"I know."

She nodded. "I have to go."

"Not yet. Take a few more minutes." He stood. "Let me show you my house."

"I—" She didn't really have an argument. "Okay. Yes, okay."

"I'll show you the backyard first." He took the lead. She followed, but her mind wasn't on the house or its furnishings except in vague awareness. Clean, uncluttered and homey, she thought.

He was talking to her but she wasn't paying attention, something about the house and the work he'd done on it, probably just words to distract her. An image flashed of him with his father. His tenderness. The pain in his eyes at being mistaken for his father's long-dead brother instead of his son.

Arianna put a hand on Joe's shoulder. He stopped, turned around, a question in his eyes.

"You take care of the world, don't you?" she asked.

He looked away.

She moved closer. She could see inside an open door to a bedroom, obviously his. A huge four-poster bed with maroon and blue bedding jumbled at the foot. The only bit of disorganization in his house.

"Who takes care of you, Joe?" she asked.

"I'm fine."

"You're no more 'fine' than I am." She leaned toward him, her eyes open, and kissed him. "Who takes care of you?"

Eight

Joe let her kiss him. Just for a minute, he thought. He would stop her in a minute.

But he didn't stop her. Couldn't— No. Didn't *want* to stop her.

He wrapped his arms around her and dragged her closer, tipping her head back, parting her lips with his, catching her sighs and moans in his mouth, a pleasure beyond his dreams. And he had been dreaming of her. Night and day. Hot, uninhibited dreams of what he would do if he had the chance.

He had the chance. Now what would he do?

It was too soon. They barely knew each other. They were both hurting. They weren't being rational. Stupid behavior led to stupid consequences.

She locked her arms around his neck and pulled herself against him. Her breasts cushioned his chest. Their abdomens melded. Her thighs pressed his, moved electrifyingly.

He slipped one thigh between hers and dragged it higher until she dropped her head back and made a long, low sound. He deepened the kiss as she went wild in his arms.

Consequences. The word rang and echoed.

Be damned. It had been so long, and she felt so good, and he needed to forget. So did she.

He backed her into his bedroom, stopped beside his bed, and looked at her.

"Yes," she whispered, her hands along his face, pulling him back to her. "Yes."

Permission in the word but a plea in her voice. Then there were no words between them, only the moment. The feel of her skin as he pulled her clothes away. The heated touch of her hands as she undressed him, explored him in the same way that he did her, in frantic haste but thoroughly. The taste of her, her spicy store-bought scent not masking the exquisite essence that was Arianna. The sounds that filtered from her chest and throat and mouth, wordless yet with so much meaning.

He'd never seen a more magnificent body, never made love with a woman who so matched him in need and strength. He acknowledged the exhilaration of finding such a rare partner as he urged her onto the bed.

Then he stopped thinking. She was there, everywhere, all around him, over, under and in him, the contact so hot they were slippery from sweat. Just as he was about to bury himself in her, she rose up, maneuvered him onto his back and climbed onto him, taking control, taking over. He let her…for the moment. How could he not? Her mouth lit fires along his skin, her hair sparked electrical charges so strong he thought he heard thunder. Her passion, her need, rained down on him until he was drowning in it.

He rolled with her, plunged into her, found a rhythm. Ah, damn, she felt good. Hot and slick and tight. Her strong legs wrapped around him, her body arched toward him. She cried out, a sound that went on and on and on as he tried to hold back. Sweat poured from him. His teeth ground. His jaw locked. His muscles seized.

A dazzling display of light and sound burst around him. Then the quiet aftermath when the display was done. Peace. Joy. Pleasure. He couldn't remember another moment remotely like it.

He became aware of the world again little by little. Arianna didn't speak. He felt her stillness as much as he would've felt her agitation. He kissed her, but she barely responded. He moved to her side. She didn't look at him.

Regret might as well have been written on her forehead.

Joe knew the moment she wanted to leave. He also knew she wouldn't want to be questioned about it, so he climbed out of bed and scooped up his clothes, then gathered hers and laid them on the bed.

He left without saying anything, dressed in the hall and waited for her on the living room sofa.

She still looked like a poster girl for unbridled sex, he thought, as she came up to him. "I have to go," she said.

He nodded. He knew. She picked up the canvas bag containing her father's file.

Joe grabbed her wrist. "I'll help you."

"Help me what?"

"Find out the truth about your father. If it's possible."

"Why would you do that?"

"Because even if you hadn't gone in search of answers to your questions, I would've found your father's file in the safe on my own. I would've felt obligated to know why it was there. What it means. I've discovered that I need answers, too, just like you."

She pulled her hand free and sat down in a chair across from him. "What kinds of answers?"

"What role my father played. Where the gun came from."

She straightened. "Are you saying—"

"I'm not saying anything. But there's a reason why he had the file locked up so that no one would find it but me— and then only on his death, he probably figured, not expecting Alzheimer's to strike first. I don't know what the reason is, but whatever it is can't be good."

"No. But how can we work together? Especially now, after having sex."

Her directness reminded him of her reputation for being unsentimental. He'd seen evidence contrary to that. Now he saw truth of it, too. Their lovemaking had apparently affected him more than her.

"Tonight I remembered something important," he said, dragging his hands down his face. "I was fourteen when your father died. I remember because it was my freshman year in high school, which sticks in your memory, and my dad was on edge for months. Mom and I tiptoed around him. He must have been investigating your father's death." In fact he'd been strung as tight as Joe had been for the past year. The parallels weren't hard to miss. Was it the case—as part of it was for Joe with the unsolved Leventhal case—or more?

"Joe." She stopped, closed her eyes for a second. "How can we work together? One of us might find out something horrible about our father. There are ethics involved here, and our individual and personal need to keep our fathers honest and upright in our memories. That kind of conflict would be hard to reconcile."

"So we should each investigate on our own? After twenty-five years and so little information to go on, how far do you think we'll get? If we put our heads and resources together, we might find something." He leaned toward her. "I may learn my father didn't do his job competently. You may learn something about your father you don't want to know. But our goal is to find the truth, isn't it? No matter what the truth is. No matter how painful."

She took a long time in answering. "Would you have told me about it, if you'd found the file before I came after the truth myself?"

"I don't know," he said honestly. "Maybe I would've explored it first, then taken it to you. It's irrelevant, Arianna. We seem destined to work together on this. To know the truth."

She cocked her head. "I never would've pegged you as a fatalist."

"Things happen. If you don't accept them and move on, you wallow in it. Blaming fate is a good enough excuse."

"It's not good to wallow," she said, the beginnings of a smile forming.

"Definitely not."

"Okay." She rubbed her hands along her thighs. "Okay. We'll partner up. The cop and the P.I. Strange bedfellows, as Scott said."

"'Strange' isn't the word I would use." Extraordinary. Incredible. Premier. For a second he thought she might blush, but she didn't. She did ignore his comment, however.

"When do you want to get started?" she asked.

"You name it. Tomorrow. Tonight. You're welcome to spend the night."

"I can't," she said instantly. "I have an early meeting and a full day. I can come after work."

"That's fine. I have plenty to do."

She stood, so he did, too. "Is everything done at your parents' house?"

"No. But it's getting there." He pointed to the packet she still clutched. "I think you should leave that here."

She pulled it tighter. "Why?"

"Because you'll stay up all night trying to make sense of it. You need some sleep."

"If I leave it, you'll do the same."

"I won't. Put it down, Arianna. It'll be safe here."

"I want to make copies of everything, just in case."

"I'll do that tomorrow." He slid it from her hands. "Get some rest. I'll have dinner for you tomorrow."

He wanted to ask her if she was okay to drive. He wanted to drive her home himself. Better yet to have her stay with him, sleep beside him. Just sleep. But he knew what her answer would be.

The moment grew more awkward. They'd made love. Shouldn't they kiss good-night? She wasn't wearing an expression that encouraged it. Ah, to hell with it. He put his arms around her and pulled her close. She didn't relax.

"I'm sorry about your dad," she said against his shoulder. "I can't imagine how hard it is on you."

"Thank you."

He let her go. After a moment she headed to the front door. She looked back over her shoulder as if she wanted to say something, then didn't. He followed her to her car. She didn't waste any time taking off. He couldn't even call to make sure she got home okay. He didn't have her phone number. He'd slept with her, but he didn't have her phone number. What kind of sense did that make?

He locked up his house, stripped off his jeans and lay facedown on his bed where he could smell her in the sheets. He fisted the fabric. Had it only been a one-night stand for her? A way to forget for a little while?

Did he want more than that, anyway? He was setting himself up for more hurt if he expected more from her. Maybe he didn't even have it in him to give.

But he wouldn't know without trying.

* * *

Arianna stayed in her shower for a long time, her eyes closed, the water pounding her back. Idiot. She'd broken her hard and fast rules. One, never get involved with someone you work with. Two, always keep control of the relationship. Three, never have unprotected sex.

Well, now what was she supposed to do? First, she'd gotten involved with a man she'd worked with in the past and would likely work with in the future in an official capacity. Just as important, she was going to work with him now—on the most important investigation of her career.

Second, she'd lost control along the way, of her actions *and* reactions. He'd not only taken charge at some point, she'd let him. Stop the presses. That was headline material for her.

Third, it was the first time she hadn't demanded a man use protection. She was on the Pill, but still....

Look what she'd done. Broken all the rules. The repercussions were bound to haunt her.

She finally turned off the shower, grabbed the towel she'd thrown over the glass door and buried her face in it. She was crazy to get involved with him. Crazy and foolish. They were both vulnerable. Not a good time to embark on a relationship, especially a risky one.

Of course, it wasn't his fault they'd slept together, but hers. So, she only had herself to blame for the consequences. The last thing she wanted was to hurt him.

Arianna dried her hair, then slipped into a T-shirt and cotton pajama bottoms. Her neighbors wouldn't appreciate her playing the piano at this hour, and it was too late to return her mother's message on her answering machine. Thank goodness. She couldn't deal with her mother tonight.

She could deal with Joe, however.

She grabbed the phone, dialed his number. He answered on the second ring.

"I hope I didn't wake you," she said.

"You didn't. I'm glad you called. Can't sleep?"

"I haven't tried yet. I needed to tell you something first."

"Okay."

She couldn't judge his tone of voice. "If we're going to work together, we need to forget tonight ever happened."

"We do?"

"Yes."

"Why's that?"

"Isn't it obvious?"

"Apparently only to you, Arianna. The way I see it, we reached out to each other. We kissed. We made love. It felt good. It felt great. Didn't it feel great?"

"Yes, but—"

"No buts. We needed each other. We met those needs. We're adults."

He didn't sound the least bit perturbed. "I've never had unprotected sex before," she said.

His hesitation seemed to stretch forever. "You're using birth control?"

"Of course."

"Of course," he repeated, a smile in his voice. "Then you have nothing to worry about."

"Okay." Which fixed only one of the three rules she'd broken. She tried to at least gain control of the relationship. "So, we're agreed we won't talk about it."

Again he was silent for several seconds, then finally said, "You can try to ignore it all you want. I choose not to."

"Meaning what?"

"I'm not going to ignore it. Or forget it. It meant something to me. Didn't it mean anything to you?"

How was she supposed to answer that? Damn him. He knew exactly how to put her on the spot. "It meant something." *I even broke my rules.* "But I'm asking you as a gentleman not to hold it against me."

He laughed.

She realized what she'd said. *Damn* him. "I meant I'm asking you not to remind me of it constantly."

"That's a promise I can't make." His voice became gentle. "Nothing that good has happened to me in a long time. I can't ignore it. But I'll leave the next move to you, if that makes you more comfortable."

He sounded a little bit smug, as if he knew she couldn't resist him. Well, she would show him. "Deal."

"Sweet dreams," he said.

"Same to you, Detective."

He laughed quietly. "Back to business, are we? Okay. By the way, in case you're wondering, what happened tonight was only a sprint."

She listened to the dial tone for several seconds before she replaced the receiver. Then she smiled.

Nine

Arianna kept her focus on the staff meeting the next morning. She had to. She ran them. After the meeting she was scheduled for an appointment with a new client in need of unobtrusive personal protection when he attended a charity ball later in the month. She'd seen a photo of him—fifty-two and easy on the eyes. He was also the target of an animal rights organization which took issue with his pharmaceutical company's use of lab animals to test potential drugs.

Whether she had an issue with that or not, she believed no one should be the victim of violence because his belief system was different. So, if she thought the setup was workable, she would take the job, even though she might get caught up in the violence herself. With her posing as his date, he would appear unconcerned about his safety, while being well guarded.

"Anything else?" Arianna asked the staff assembled in the conference room as business wound down.

No one added anything. They wandered out of the room, several of them stopping to grab another bagel or muffin. Laughter punctuated the steady hum of conversation. She, Sam and Nate hired well. The group was congenial and collegial. They had differences of opinion, some of them strong, but those differences were respected, and the years of experience each person brought to the company meant they needed little direct supervision. Arianna loved going to work.

Except for today. Today she wished she were at Joe's house, analyzing his father's notes.

She noticed Sam lingering after the room had emptied. "Any luck locating Doc?" she asked.

"We're playing phone tag." He cocked his head. "You were a little off today."

"Long day yesterday." She gathered her paperwork and stood.

"Is that all?"

He watched her closely, but as a friend, with concern in his eyes.

"Does it have something to do with Joe Vicente?" Sam pressed.

She leaned a hip against the table. "He's going to help me try to find my father's killer." She explained the basics. "I have to make the effort," she said finally.

He nodded. "If there's anything I can do, let me know."

The receptionist, Julie, appeared in the doorway. "Arianna, Joe Vicente is on line three, and I just put your mother in your office."

Her mother? Here? She'd come to Arianna's office probably three times in all the years they'd been in business. "Thank you, Julie."

"Want me to go?" Sam asked.

"No. Hang on a sec." She punched the line-three button. "Good morning, Detective."

"Hi. How'd you sleep?"

"Great, thanks. What can I do for you?"

"Ah. All business. Okay. Well, I've been going through the file, and I thought you might want to get a head start on tracking down the eyewitness. You have more resources than I do, since I don't have access to my work computer."

"Good idea. What's the info?"

"Mary Beth Maxwell. Age twenty-five then." He gave her the address, birth date and Social Security number.

"Thanks. Anything else I should know?"

"Not at this moment. I'll see you tonight."

"Around six, okay?"

"Sure. Bye."

After she hung up she made a copy of the information and passed it to Sam. "Would you work your magic and see if you can come up with anything on this woman? She would be fifty years old today. Could've been married and remarried a bunch of times by now. May not even be alive." Which would be another clue that went nowhere, and maybe a clue they shouldn't pursue the investigation, after all.

"I'll get right on it," Sam said. "What's Paloma doing here?"

"Being nosy, I suspect."

"A mother's prerogative, she would say. I'll stop by your office in a few minutes to say hi."

"Interrupt me with something that needs my immediate attention, okay?"

He smiled. "As mothers go, she's a good one."

"I know. I'm just not in the mood."

"Your detective a little harder to manage than you expected?"

She looked sharply at him. "What do you mean by that?"

"I've always wondered how you would react when you met your match. Now I see. You're defensive."

"I am not." She grinned, hoping to throw him off course.

He didn't take the bait. "See you in a few."

Arianna headed for her office. "Mom! What a nice surprise." She dropped her paperwork on her desk then hugged her mother. "What brings you here?"

"You didn't return my call."

"I got home too late."

"And this morning? Up and gone too early, I suppose." Paloma took a seat on the sofa. The knuckles on her clenched hands were white.

"That's right." Arianna joined her, noting the stress on her face, as well.

"So? Did you meet him?"

"Yes."

"What did he tell you?"

"Nothing."

Her mother looked at her lap. "I told you," she said.

"It wasn't that he had nothing new to tell me. Maybe he would have. But he has Alzheimer's, Mom. He's in a care home. His memory is gone, for the most part."

Was that relief on her mother's face?

"So now you'll let it drop?"

Arianna leaned forward. She put her hands over her mother's. "I can't. Not yet. There are still facts to check and clues to follow. I won't spend the rest of my life searching, if that's what you mean. But it's what I need to do now."

Paloma searched her daughter's eyes. "All right, *mija*. I will save my breath."

"Thank you. You know, it was really odd seeing Mr. Vicente. I had a flashback of when he came to the house after Dad died. You screamed at him. And he was so kind—to both of us."

Paloma stiffened. "He had a job to do. He wasn't doing it well enough or fast enough for me."

"In the end he didn't do it at all. They never found the killer."

"Hey, gorgeous." Sam came into the room.

Her mother transformed as Sam bent down to kiss her cheek, her expression changing from pinched to pleased, the contrast making Arianna even more starkly aware of how much her mother was upset by Arianna digging for information. She couldn't help that, however. Her need to know took priority.

"How was your honeymoon?" Paloma asked Sam.

"Everything a honeymoon should be." He looked at Arianna. "I thought you had an appointment."

She looked at her watch. "I do. Mom, I've really got to run."

Arianna walked her mother to her car. Going with her gut instinct, Arianna asked, "Is there something you're not telling me?"

"There is a great deal I haven't told you, *mija*." Her smile was serene.

"About Dad. About his murder. Are you afraid of something that might come out if I investigate too closely?"

"I am worried about you. Do not let it become an obsession."

Which wasn't an answer, Arianna thought, but she let it go. For now.

Arianna made it through the day. She accepted the case

to do personal protection for the pharmaceutical CEO. She met with two other clients regarding ongoing cases. Sam hadn't had any luck locating the eyewitness, Mary Beth Maxwell, as yet.

Arianna changed into jeans and a peasant blouse in her office then went to her car. She hit the speakerphone button and dialed Joe's number to tell him she was on her way.

"Could you pick up a loaf of bread and a gallon of milk on the way?" he asked.

"Um, sure."

He laughed. "I was kidding. I've been feeling like a housewife waiting for her husband to come home."

"Oh." She smiled. "Vacation getting to you?"

"It got to me on the first day. But I'm getting better. See you soon. Bring your appetite. I've been slaving away all day."

She'd never been wooed before. Well, some had tried, she had to admit, but she had no interest in being courted. "You promised that the next move was mine."

"There are moves, and then there are moves."

She heard the confident smile in his voice. Smart. She liked that about him. And quick. And attractive. And an amazing sprinter. She'd known from his first kiss that it would be good between them—he knew how to make the most of a moment—still she'd been surprised by the intensity.

"I have a feeling you can find a fix for any complication," she said.

"You think? See you soon. Drive safe."

"Always," she said, then ended the call, suddenly in a much better mood.

Contrary to what Joe had told Arianna, he hadn't been slaving in the kitchen all day. He planned to grill hamburgers, and he'd bought salad and dessert from a local deli. She would probably be horrified at the fat and calorie content, but his repertoire of culinary accomplishments was a short list.

The phone rang. He wondered if she was calling to say she wouldn't be able to make it, after all.

It wasn't Arianna, however, but his lieutenant returning his call.

"You wanted me to check in once in a while," Joe said.

"How's it going?" Morgan asked.

"Good."

"You keeping busy?"

"Yeah."

"How's your father?"

"The same. I'm almost done clearing out the house. The new owners take possession next week."

"So, it'll be behind you."

Only someone who hadn't been through what he'd been through would say it like that, like it was easy to give up your history. "Yeah."

"Been on a date?"

"As a matter of fact, yes." He couldn't have asked for a better lead into what he wanted to ask Morgan. "With Arianna Alvarado."

"The P.I.?"

"We met at a Halloween party. Did you know her father was LAPD and was killed on the job?" He saw Arianna's car pull up in front of his house.

"I did know that. She doesn't seem like your type."

"I was surprised, too. What's the story with her father, do you know? She says it's unsolved and my dad was lead on it." Joe opened the front door as Arianna came up the walkway. She smiled and walked past him then on into the living room. He was distracted by the way she looked in her jeans, so he didn't notice Morgan's silence until several seconds had passed.

"I remember when the shooting took place," Morgan said. "But I wasn't a detective yet."

"I'd like to come in and take a look at the file."

A few beats passed. "I told you four weeks and I meant it, Joe."

"This would be different."

"No, it would be another obsession in your life."

"Are you saying I can't see the file?"

Arianna raised her brows at him.

"I'm saying I don't want to see you anywhere near this building. Let it go."

"I might be able to, but I doubt she will. Just so you know."

"Thanks for the warning. And thanks for the call. I'm glad you're making good use of your time off, although I have to say, I can't picture you with Ms. Alvarado."

"She's not as tough as her reputation."

"Maybe. Keep me up to date."

Joe pressed the off button. He tossed the phone to his other hand and back again. "Interesting."

"What was?"

He put the phone aside and sat beside her on the sofa. "My lieutenant pretty much told me not to get involved in your father's case."

"He forbid you?"

"More like warned me off."

"What do you think it means?"

"That there's more to the story."

Her eyes darkened. "There's no way we can get the official file and see if there's anything different there?"

"Not without permission. And you can bet I can't get

permission now. Morgan probably put a freeze on it in Records.''

"He can do that?''

"I don't see why not.''

"Even with the Freedom of Information Act, I couldn't get it now?''

"I don't know. We'd have to check. But at least we have the photocopies of the file, and something the official record doesn't have—my father's notes.''

"Indecipherable, but there,'' she said. She stood. "Let's get started.''

He stood, too. Keeping his hands off her took willpower. "Dinner first.''

"But—''

He shook his head. "Dinner. Conversation. A little relaxation. Then we'll work.''

"I'm not hungry.''

"Then you can keep me company while I eat. I know you're anxious, but you also need fuel.''

"*You* are bossy.''

He led the way to the backyard, to the barbecue. "Just making sure you don't fall into the same trap as I did.''

"What trap?''

"I didn't take time for myself this past year. Not only did it wear me out and burn me out, I lost a fiancée because of it.''

Ten

Finally, Arianna thought. She would learn about his fiancée. "What was her name?" she asked.

"Jane." He lifted the lid on the barbecue and shoved the hot coals around with some tongs, making an even layer.

"I hope you like hamburgers."

She smiled. He'd been teasing her about the food. "Yes."

"And potato salad?"

"Homemade?"

"Made by someone." He grinned. "And raspberry cheesecake. Made by someone."

"So, you slaved all day, hmm?" *Can we end the banter and get to the issue of your fiancée?*

"Hey, it took me hours to decide what to buy. It's the thought that counts."

"It is." She wandered away from him, waiting him out. A koi pond sat to one side of a slate path. Several koi scooted into a dark corner as she approached. She sat on a wooden bench to watch. "This is a beautiful spot. Did you add the pond?"

"Came with the house, but I had to fix it up." He went silent. "It's killing you, not asking questions," he said finally.

She turned her head toward him. As he added the hamburger patties, smoke and sizzle rose from the grill, obscuring him. "I admit I'm curious."

"Want a beer?"

Another stall, she thought. "That'd be great."

He went into the house. She stared into the water. Oh, he was a cool one. He could draw out a discussion until the average person would be ready to punch him. She wasn't average, however. She hoped he knew that.

When he returned he passed her a bottle and sat beside her. She took a swallow, then waited, aware of him next to her. She remembered how he kissed, a slow heat that turned blazing hot. She remembered how his mouth felt on her breast, and the feel of his body on hers. And how he felt inside her....

"We met at a Lakers game," he said. "Two years ago."

"She's a basketball fan?"

"She's employed by the team."

"A cheerleader?" Arianna, who'd never known a moment of jealousy, suddenly felt it rise up inside her. She didn't like the feeling.

"Public relations."

"You fell in love."

After a few seconds he nodded. "We got engaged about a month before my mother was diagnosed with cancer."

Arianna waited.

"Jane hung in there for a few months, but she got fed up with me putting my parents first. Plus it was the busiest time of year for her. She was on the road a lot with the team. Then there were the play-offs. She expected me to ignore my parents when she was in town. I couldn't…. She gave me back the ring. That was six months ago.''

''Your mother died a month later.''

He nodded.

''Then your father was alone, and you stepped in.''

''I don't regret it.''

''Yet you lost your fiancée because of it.''

''Obviously it wasn't a good match.''

''She was selfish.''

He got up and went to the barbecue to flip the burgers. ''She deserved more than I could give her.''

Arianna decided not to comment. She was glad he was rid of Jane, who apparently hadn't loved him enough to share his burdens.

''How about you?'' he asked. ''Any former fiancés?''

''I've never even contemplated marriage.'' *Never been in love. Never cared about anything more than my work.* ''Between the job and what I have to do to keep myself in shape for it, I don't even have time for dating much. Every week I've got yoga classes and tae kwon do, plus I go to the shooting range. And I'm the managing partner in the firm. That means more hours in the office than anyone else.''

''Do you travel a lot?''

''Quite a bit, but not as much as Nate and Sam. I have to keep the office running.''

''Do you own a house?''

''No. I've been thinking about it, but I like the apartment where I live. It's close to the office and large enough for my needs.'' She'd been craving a house lately, though. A place where she could play piano at midnight if she wanted. A place where she could plant a few flowers— Well, maybe not. A place where she could hire a gardener, anyway. She smiled at the thought.

Over dinner they talked about their childhoods and high school. First jobs. First sweethearts. She relaxed, more than she had since she'd first set the course to find out the truth about her father's murder.

The air cooled as night set in. They carried the dishes inside then sat at his dining room table, where he'd stacked the paperwork.

"Here are your copies," he said, shoving a pile toward her. "I ran a set for myself, too, so we'll keep the originals fresh. I also made a list of the facts I know based on the file. Plus I spent a lot of time today going through his notebooks from other cases, trying to decipher the abbreviations he used in this one."

"Were you able to?" she asked, scanning the list of facts he'd given her.

"No."

She looked up. "Not at all?"

"He did abbreviate things, but not anything like the numbers and letters that are scattered throughout his notes about your father, which seemed to be more like a personal code."

"Another dead end," Arianna said, discouraged. And an even bigger question. What was he hiding?

"Are you prepared to accept that you may not find any answers?" Joe asked.

She considered his question. "If I say no, you might think I don't have faith in your father's ability to investigate. If I say yes, you might think I'm going to give up soon. There is no right answer to that question. For now, I just want to double-check and follow through and see what we find. If all we find are dead ends, so be it." Maybe.

She was afraid her nightmares wouldn't end unless she found the truth.

"Fair enough. Okay, so what we know for sure is that there was only one eyewitness, Mary Beth Maxwell, who was the clerk on duty at the liquor store where your father was killed during a robbery. She was shot three times and spent weeks in the hospital recovering."

"According to her statement," Arianna added, "she had no clear memory of the event. She came to in the hospital two days after the surgery that saved her life. The cash register was empty. Best guess by the owner is that they got away with a few hundred dollars. Not worth shooting anyone for, especially since she didn't have a weapon, but my father probably drew his and the killers fired before being fired upon, then shot Mary Beth so there would be no witnesses."

"Right. That much is pretty straightforward. She was shot with a .22 caliber. He was shot with a .38."

"I'm sure those weapons are long gone now."

"I imagine so. But take a look at page seven. It says your father's gun—a .38 caliber, police issue at the time— was never found at the scene."

"Do you think it's the one in your father's safe?"

"Maybe. Can't prove it one way or the other. They didn't do ballistics tracings on the issued weapons in those days like they do now."

They worked for hours, recording combinations of letters, finding where they were repeated and seeing if they fit in any other context. Arianna's almost sleepless night before caught up with her. Even though it was only ten o'clock, she was exhausted. And totally aware of Joe's presence, solid, calm and...tempting. Every time she lost patience with the process, he settled her down by diverting her or pointing out something else. He touched her, too.

His hands bumped hers when they reached for a paper at the same time. Or he gave her a quick shoulder massage each time he left the room to get something to drink or look up something on the Internet.

Like a friend, Arianna decided. An old, comfortable friend—who also turned her on. The massage may have seemed friendly, but as his thumbs worked the muscles in her shoulders, his fingers rested along her collarbones, sometimes drifting down just a little farther, his fingertips not quite grazing the neckline of her blouse, before he walked away.

She could've stopped him, but she didn't even try. There are moves, and then there are *moves,* he'd said. The man had *moves.* Subtle. Sure. Scintillating.

She sighed.

"What?" he asked.

"Nothing."

He looked squarely at her. "You're tired."

It was partially true. "Yes. I should probably go home."

"Stay."

"I can't."

"Yes, you can. I have a guest room. You're too tired to drive."

He was right, of course. So why was she balking? Because she'd never let anyone tell her what to do since she'd left the army? Undoubtedly it was more complicated than that. "Don't get paternal on me, Detective."

He just smiled.

"I do have a change of clothes in my car," she said casually.

"I'll get the room ready while you get your stuff."

Apparently the decision was made.

She met him in the guest room then set down the overnight bag she always kept in her trunk, along with a suit and blouse.

She glanced around the room. An old-fashioned quilt covered the bed, although the furniture looked new. The room was appealing in its simplicity, like the rest of the house.

"The bed looks comfortable," she said.

"If it isn't, you can join me in mine."

She shook her head, smiling. "You don't give up."

"Not this time. Do you need anything?"

"I don't have anything to wear to bed. A T-shirt would be great."

He left. She ran her hand over the quilt, discovering it was hand-stitched. She blew out a breath. She hadn't been this nervous around a man for as long as she could remember.

When he came back he held a light blue dress shirt with long sleeves. "I wanted to picture you in this instead." He tossed it to her. "Good night."

"G'night." She waited until she heard his bedroom door shut before she walked down the hall to the bathroom. After a quick shower she dressed in the shirt then made her way back to the bedroom. The shirt felt like a hug. The sheets were cool. The house was quiet. Too quiet. She must have gotten her second wind, because she wasn't the least bit sleepy.

After tossing and turning for a while she got out of bed and went to the kitchen for a glass of water. Glass in hand, she wandered down the hall to the French doors that opened to the backyard. Moonlight bathed the yard and reflected off the pond. If it'd been summer she would've let herself outside to enjoy the evening. Instead she stood and watched and waited, as if something were about to happen.

Nothing did. If she wanted something to happen, she had to make it happen, not wait for it.

She took her glass to the guest room and set it on a coaster on the nightstand. She sat on the edge of the bed. She didn't want to go to sleep. She didn't want the nightmares about her father to return.

After a few minutes of staring at her feet she left the room again, this time heading to the master bedroom. She expected the door to be closed, but it wasn't. She stopped and listened. No sleeping sounds at all. No snoring, or even heavy breathing.

She moved into the room, not making a sound. She could see from his silhouette that he was on his back. She slowed down as she neared him. Suddenly he turned his head slightly and looked at her. She stopped, held her breath.

He lifted the comforter invitingly.

She slid into his bed and his arms, which wrapped around her and tucked the comforter tight at the same time. She burrowed against him. What was it about him that weakened her—and why didn't she mind? He already carried the weight of the world on his shoulders, and she didn't want to add to it, yet he didn't make her feel like a burden.

She breathed his name.

"Sleep," he said. "Just sleep."

She thought she should warn him. "I have nightmares."

"I have insomnia."

"Oh. Well. Good. At least I won't wake you up."

He laughed softly, his breath warm against her hair. She settled more comfortably against him. It wasn't working, however. She wasn't sleepy. She wanted him.

"Have I told you how much I admire your mind?" she said.

"I'd rather you admire my butt."

She laughed. "I do. But I'm happy that we're working well together as a team."

"So am I. Go to sleep."

"Why? I can't be keeping you awake."

He rubbed his chin against her hair, but she figured he was smiling at least.

She was pretty sure he wore boxer shorts or something similar. Her knee had brushed fabric when he'd first drawn her close. She wondered if he usually slept in the nude.

She toyed with the hair on his chest. "Do you think, since we've already been intimate, that we could handle a physical relationship as part of our partnership?"

He was quiet for several seconds. "Do you?"

"Would I have asked otherwise?"

"If you wanted to tease me."

"I don't. Want to tease you." She leaned back a little, just enough to see his face in the dark.

"Let's talk about it tomorrow," he said.

Disappointment swamped her. "Tomorrow?"

"When saner heads prevail."

The man had willpower. But considering that she'd instigated what happened last night, she thought she should wait for him this time. After a minute she couldn't come up with anything more to say, so she tucked herself against him again and closed her eyes.

"I can't believe you bought that," he said, propping himself up on an elbow, laughter in his voice. He brushed the hair from her face. "You really think I'd pass up the opportunity to make love with you?" He leaned toward her.

She put her hand over his mouth. "There's an undeniable attraction between us I figure is going to make it hard to work together if we don't have an outlet for it. And it's critical that we work well together, because what we find may be hard to face." She took her hand away. "If sleeping

together keeps some of the tension out of the working relationship, then I'm all for it. If you agree.''

''Sounds good to me.'' He brushed his lips against hers.

She wondered if she should tell him that as soon as they
were done with the investigation, the relationship would be
done, too. No. Her reasons would sound egotistical. He was
obviously ready for a family of his own. She wasn't. Would
probably never be. He was a cop, and cops were notorious
for having bad track records with relationships. She'd seen
it for herself with her parents, whose relationship was so
different from those of her friends' parents. If Arianna ever
made a commitment, it had to be a partnership in every
sense of the word, the good and the bad.

But if she voiced her reasons out loud, it would sound
like she expected him to fall in love with her. She didn't
expect that. His ex-fiancée's career got in the way of their
relationship. Arianna's would, too. She had to remember
that, too, to guard herself. He would be an easy man to get
serious about.

So she left it alone and kissed him back, savoring the
slow tenderness he offered this time as opposed to last
night's impetuous and intense coupling.

His lips were warm and firm and made her hunger for
more. His tongue found hers and stroked leisurely, thoroughly, enticingly. His hands moved down her body, leaving a trail of heat. Buttons came undone. The shirt came
off. Then he was naked, too, and slipping a leg between
hers. He dragged his mouth down her neck and over her
collarbone, lifting her breast with his hand to meet his open
mouth. Her nipple ached until he drew it into the wet heat,
his tongue circling, teeth scraping before closing his lips
and sucking it deeply.

She rose up. He held her down. She moaned. He encouraged her. His tempo picked up. Searching. Seeking.

Finding. Satisfying. Oh, he knew what to do. But first she had things to do to him.

He didn't fight it for long. She welcomed the freedom to taste him. Touch him. Please him. She liked that she could draw deep-chested sounds from him, rumbles of arousal, rough whispers of encouragement. She lingered, enjoying herself, enjoying his reaction. She explored his bold contours, savored the unrelenting heat and strength. Triumphed when he called her name, pleasure and pain in the sound. He was as out of control as she'd been last night. It excited her even more, knowing what she was doing to him.

Suddenly he dove his fingers into her hair and dragged her up. He devoured her mouth with his. She let go of any remaining trace of restraint to just feel. She felt his hands cup her rear and lift her higher, pushing himself deeper, moving faster, harder. The pleasure built impossibly stronger but wouldn't peak. She wrapped her legs around him. He kissed her, his tongue thrusting in rhythm.

Then there was no more buildup but a huge burst that lasted and lasted and lasted. He didn't hold back, either, but joined her, their slick bodies slamming against each other, the sex-scented air humid and thick. Finally he slowed, stopped, draped himself over her. She tried to breathe. Tried to come up with a coherent thought. A thought came but couldn't be articulated.

"That was the one-mile race," he said close to her ear.

She laughed, a short, out-of-breath sound. "I think you broke a record."

"I think *we* did." He rolled to his side, taking her with him. "Will you spend your nights here from now on?"

"Yes." *Until our job is done.*

"Good." He drew her against him, kissed her hair. "Sleep now."

"I need a shower now."

"Want your back washed?"

"That would be nice."

In the shower he showed her he could pole vault, too. She wished she had a gold medal to give him.

Eleven

The next afternoon Joe drove by Mary Beth Maxwell's house, continued around the block again, then parked a few houses up the street from hers. She was Mary Beth Horvath now, having married Leon Horvath nineteen years ago. They had two teenage sons. Arianna's partner Sam Remington had tracked down the eyewitness to Mateo Alvarado's murder to a quiet street in middle-class Fullerton, where they had lived for twelve years.

Barely an hour ago Arianna had called Joe to pass on the information. He volunteered to do a little surveillance but would not approach Mary Beth until Arianna could be there, too. They wouldn't make an appointment, either, the element of surprise generally giving them an advantage. But if they couldn't catch her at home alone, they would have to call and schedule a time.

He studied the surroundings, wondering how long it would take for a curious neighbor to notice him and either approach and ask what he was doing or call the police directly. A Neighborhood Watch sign was visible from where he sat.

A red Ford Explorer, one of three cars registered to the Horvath family, pulled into the driveway. A woman got out, average height and weight. Attractive. Blond. She gathered a few shopping bags from the back seat and headed into the house. In a few minutes she came back for more then pressed the car alarm button on her key chain and returned to the house.

Joe waited. Twenty minutes later a blue VW Beetle convertible, also registered to the Horvaths, pulled in next to the Explorer. Four teenage boys exited the car and disappeared into the house, backpacks in tow, two of the teens tossing a basketball between them.

A half hour later, three of the boys came out the front door. Two got in the car. The third, the driver, opened his door then stopped and looked in Joe's direction. He said something to the other boys. They got out of the car and ambled up to Joe's car, as if being in a group would save them from being shot, if that was what Joe intended. Kids.

"What're you doin'?" the driver asked. Tall, skinny and belligerent, he was a typical teen.

Joe flashed his detective shield. "Surveillance."

"Cool," one of the other boys said. "Who you lookin' at?"

"I can't say."

"Bet it's—"

The Horvath kid elbowed him into silence. "Your badge says L.A., not Fullerton. Can you be here?"

"Yes. And, boys, you're making it kind of hard to stay unobtrusive."

"It's cool," one kid said, grabbing the Horvath boy's arm and pulling him along.

They sent a few backward glances in Joe's direction. The Horvath boy sent a particularly long look, probably memorizing Joe's license plate.

When Mr. Horvath hadn't shown up by six o'clock, Joe left to meet Arianna at home. Her car was already parked in the driveway.

He wondered if he could kiss her hello. She had managed to avoid a kiss goodbye that morning, as if the bedroom was the only place they would touch, the physical relationship to be kept separate from their working one.

He'd missed her all day. He hated admitting that to himself, but he had. She'd had a violent nightmare during the night, and he'd held and soothed her until she fell back asleep. He'd been glad he was there.

But he'd also slept, surprisingly. Better than he had in months. And his stomach had calmed down since he'd started vacation.

Since he'd met her.

He opened his front door and stopped. Something smelled incredible.

He followed the smell into the kitchen, where Arianna was working some kind of magic on the stove.

"You cook," he said.

"You can thank my mother."

"I will." He moved closer, intending to kiss her.

She held up a spoon loaded with a rice mixture. "Taste."

So, no kiss. He ate the food from the spoon. "Good," he said. Then fire attacked his mouth and tongue. He grabbed the faucet, turned on the cold water and angled his head to get a mouthful of water. "That's some kick," he said, breathing hard, his eyes watering.

"I figured you were up to it, Detective."

Yeah, but not his stomach. Maybe if he filled it with beer first, so it had a place to land and dilute. "What's in that?"

"Rice and beans. Chilis. Hot ones."

"No—" he coughed "—kidding. The flavor's unbelievable, though."

She smiled. "I've been marinating chicken in a lime and tequila mix. I started the coals a while ago, if you'd like to grill the chicken."

"Sure."

"But first, what'd you find out?"

As he grabbed a beer to cool his still-on-fire mouth, he related what he'd seen. "I couldn't tell from her clothes if she'd been working or just out doing errands, but we can go in the morning and see if we can catch her alone. Can you arrange your schedule to do that?"

"I already did."

"Okay." He took the bag of marinated chicken from her and grabbed some tongs. "Don't expect miracles, Arianna. If she couldn't remember then, she probably couldn't add to it now."

"I know."

He wondered if she did. He was afraid that her hopes were unrealistically high. All he could do was continue to caution her.

They ate in the backyard again, by the koi pond. It was the best meal he could remember having—at least of the non-comfort-food variety. After having cool lime sorbet for dessert they went back to work on the files.

"Don't you think it's strange that there was only one eyewitness?" Arianna asked after a while. "The liquor store was in a busy part of town. It was noon. Doesn't that seem odd that the store was empty?"

"Yeah. I've wondered about that, too. And his partner was up the street buying them sandwiches for lunch, heard the shots but was too late to see the shooters."

''No one else saw them, either.'' She drummed her pen on the table. ''That's hard to believe.''

Because the official reports told only the facts, there was no speculation from Joe's father. He must have thought it odd, too, though. Joe thumbed through the copies of the notebook looking for any mention of the lack of witnesses, something Joe would include in his own notes on his cases—speculation, theories, ideas that went nowhere but needed to be ruled out.

''What was his partner's name?'' Arianna asked.

''Fred Zamora.''

''FZ. Z. I've seen that letter alone in the notes. I thought it was a 2, which totally confused me. Have you seen it?'' She hunted through the papers.

''Yeah. I thought it was a 2, too.'' He checked his list of codes he'd culled from the notes, then spun the paper toward her. ''It's on these pages.''

She gave him a flirty look. ''I do like an organized man.''

He wanted to kiss her. Ached to kiss her. Her look of intense concentration all evening had made him smile more than once. And the hint of cleavage he could see from across the table made him wish the clock would fast forward to bedtime. She was focused *and* sexy without trying. The one-two punch packed a wallop.

They looked at each of the seven pages with a Z on it, from the day of the murder to a month later, but the letters that followed the Z made no sense to Arianna or Joe.

''We need to contact this guy,'' she said. ''I'll ask Sam. It'll be a little more difficult without his pertinent numbers, like a birth date.''

''He probably played a prominent role at the funeral. We'll watch the tape again and see if we can spot him.

Estimate his age. I don't suppose your mother would offer any information?"

"I doubt it. I can ask, though."

"You don't remember him at all?"

"Maybe if I saw him, I would. It was so long ago."

"Yeah. Even if you could get an approximate age, it would help in eliminating other men with the same name."

"Can't be too many Fred Zamoras out there." She stretched and yawned. "I think I've gone as far as I can go tonight. How about you?"

He was good for another hour, but he didn't think time was going to help much. The codes were hard to break, seemingly without any rhyme or reason. If the Z did indeed represent Zamora, that was their first bit of luck. But he also didn't want to spend every hour working on it. He was supposed to be taking back his life. He intended to.

Have a normal life. He wasn't sure he knew what that was anymore, except that he knew Arianna could easily become as obsessed as he'd been. He needed to make sure that didn't happen, that she didn't end up in the kind of shape he'd been in, was still in, to some degree.

"Why don't you go relax in a hot bath," he said.

"I'm fine."

"I didn't say you weren't."

"You didn't have to say it. You implied it."

"Now you can read my mind?"

She laughed. "That would be helpful."

"There's nothing on my mind that would shock you."
Except how often I'd like to strip you naked and—

"I wonder," she said, then stood. She met his gaze. "I'd like to see the crime scene tomorrow."

"A lot will have changed in twenty-five years."

She nodded. "I need to."

"Yeah. I would, too. Go take your bath."

He took a quick shower himself, then waited for her in bed.

He heard her pad barefoot down the hall, just the sound arousing him. Then she was in his bed, all warm and dewy. Naked. Kissing him. The force of her passion staggered him until he caught up with her, then took control, giving her more than she asked for, taking as much as she would give.

"I need—" she said, breathless, after he'd entered her.

He'd been waiting, hoping, she would say something. Anything to let him know what she was feeling beyond the physical. "What do you need?" He stopped moving.

"You," she breathed. "You."

"You've got me."

"All of you."

"What more is there?" He'd left the light on this time so that he could see her. He saw her brows furrow. The skin over her cheekbones was taut and flushed. Her eyes were fathomless.

"I don't know," she said. "Something."

He started to move again. Slow. Steady. "This?"

She reached to cup his face, her gaze locked with his. She nodded.

He knew there was more she wanted to say, but she either couldn't or wouldn't. He decided not to press the point but just to please her. And to find pleasure himself.

Later, in the deep dark hours of the night, after he'd calmed her after another nightmare, he regretted not forcing her hand, and hoped there would be another opportunity to ask.

Then he slept.

Within ARC Arianna was known for her interviewing skills. Body language was her second language. Nate and Sam almost always had her sit in during interviews because of her extraordinary ability to read the slightest nuances. It was an art as well as a science, and she was a master.

Today she felt like a novice. Her stomach lurched as she and Joe pulled up in front of Mary Beth Horvath's house. She was grateful he was along and could take over if she faltered, even though the idea of him seeing her falter made her sick.

"No car in the driveway," she said.

"Maybe it's in the garage."

He opened his door. She was glad he didn't offer an encouraging little pep talk but assumed she would be professional, no matter how much emotional turmoil swirled around her. *Score another one for you, Joe Vicente.* A lot of men would've shown concern about her doing her job. He seemed to expect her to do her job. His faith settled her.

The woman who answered the door was as Joe had described yesterday.

"Mrs. Horvath?" Arianna said.

"What?" She had the impatient look of a person who figured she was going to have to say "No, thank you," to whatever they were selling and close the door in their faces.

"My name is Arianna Alvarado. This is Detective Joe Vicente of the LAPD. Could we have a few minutes of your time, please?"

Joe showed his badge and ID. Arianna didn't want to identify herself as a P.I., so she didn't show anything, letting Joe's ID cover both of them.

"I—" Mary Beth stopped. Stared. "Alvarado?"

"Mateo Alvarado was my father."

Mary Beth's face blanched.

"And Detective Mike Vicente is mine," Joe added. "May we come inside?"

After endless seconds she backed away, opening the

door, then shut it behind them with a soft click. "This way."

The house was beautifully decorated in a French country motif, Arianna noted. Tasteful but not overly formal. It was a good house for entertaining business associates while not being intimidating to teenagers who wanted to put their feet on the furniture.

Mary Beth gestured toward the sofa, inviting them to sit. She perched on a blue upholstered chair.

"Are we alone?" Joe asked.

"Yes. My children are in school. My husband is at work." She closed her eyes for a few seconds. "I thought that part of my life was over," she said. "I guess it won't die until I do."

"I'm sorry to resurrect painful memories, Mrs. Horvath," Arianna said. "We're trying to piece together what happened to my father."

She frowned. "What can I say that's different from what's in the reports?"

"I don't know. That's why we're here."

She leaned back, resigned. "All right."

"All I know for sure is that he had stopped at the liquor store where you worked to get a pack of cigarettes during his lunch break and got caught in the crossfire of a hold-up. And that you were the only witness."

"Then you also know that I was critically wounded and almost died. I can't remember much of what happened after seeing your father come in."

"For cigarettes?" Joe asked.

"And a soda. He'd headed to the refrigerator to get it. I was ringing him up. The cash drawer was open. There were two men. I didn't see them until I heard the first shot, and I don't know who shot first. I never saw their faces. After that it's a blur. More shots fired. I don't know whose or how many. I was shot. It was unreal. I remember falling against some bottles behind the counter. The next thing I knew, I woke up in the hospital with three gunshot wounds, barely alive. I was told the surgeons operated on me for nine hours.''

"I'm so sorry," Arianna said, real sympathy in her voice.

She looked at Arianna oddly then simply said thanks.

"Was the liquor store in his patrol area?" Joe asked.

"I would assume so." She plucked at some lint on the chair arm, smoothed out her face and waited.

Something's off, Arianna thought. Either Mary Beth remembered more than she was telling or she was lying about something.

"Did you go back to work there?" Joe asked.

"Of course not."

"Were you mad that the case never went to trial?"

"Mad? Why would I be? The bastard got what he deserved."

Arianna's throat closed. She didn't look at Joe, but she could guess how he was reacting to that bit of news—the same way she was. "Got what he deserved?" Arianna managed to ask.

"Well, yeah. He killed a cop. He shot me. He deserved to die."

When Arianna couldn't formulate a question, Joe took over.

"Can you tell us what you know about that?"

The woman crossed her legs, bounced her foot. "Like you can't read about it?"

A tough side of her had emerged. Arianna wondered how much she'd changed herself to fit the world she lived in now.

"I'd like to hear what you know," Joe said.

"I don't know much. They found him. He was shot dead."

"They?"

"The cops."

"The cops shot him?" Joe pressed.

"I don't know who shot him. I'm just glad he died."

"What was his name?" Arianna asked.

"No one ever told me."

"You didn't ask?"

"I saw no need to. I danced a jig and that was that. Look, is that it?" She glanced anxiously toward the front door. "Sometimes my sons come home for lunch. I don't want to explain who you are."

Arianna didn't either, and she knew the one boy could identify Joe. She needed to get out of the house and try to make sense of what she'd just learned. She gave the woman a card with her cell phone number on it. "If you think of anything else, please call me."

"Sure." She tucked it in her pocket without looking. At the door she stopped Arianna from leaving. "I was sorry about your dad. He was a nice man. You were just a little girl. I'm sorry for my part in it."

"Thank you," Arianna said, grateful for her kindness.

"Do you remember my father?" Joe asked.

She nodded. "You look a lot like him. He was okay, too."

"Thank you for your time," Arianna said.

She and Joe didn't speak. They drove until Joe pulled into a grocery store parking lot and turned off the engine.

"The case is solved," she said, fury and pain squeezing her throat, knotting her stomach. "They lied. Everyone lied. Even my mother. The case is solved. Why wouldn't they tell me? What's going on? What is in that file that they didn't want me to see?" When Joe just stared out the windshield, she pushed on, struck by something Mary Beth had said at the end. "Something's off with Mrs. Horvath. What did she mean she was sorry for her part in it?"

After a minute he looked at her. "I agree that something's off. There's more to the story. Maybe more with your dad. But with mine, too."

"Like what?" Although she knew what he would say. She knew. She just didn't want to say it first.

"I think my father might have been involved in a cover-up."

Twelve

"**A** damned cover-up," Joe repeated, stunned. He couldn't wrap the possibility around what he knew about the down-to-earth man of integrity who had raised him.

"Don't jump to conclusions," Arianna said, sounding a little shell-shocked herself.

"Right." He let go of his death grip on the steering wheel and sat back. "I need to find out who the gun in Dad's safe belonged to." He studied her. Color was returning to her face. "I don't know what to say. I hadn't anticipated anything of importance coming out of that interview."

She nodded. He slipped a hand under her hair, along her neck and brushed his thumb along her cool skin, as much for his comfort as hers.

"So many lies, Joe."

"There must be a reason why."

"If that's true, then today would just be tip-of-the-iceberg lies. How many more are there?"

Because it was a rhetorical question, he didn't answer. She closed her eyes and tipped her head forward, giving him better access to rub her neck and shoulders. "Want to go home?" he asked after a minute.

"No." She lifted her head, ending the massage. "I want to see the crime scene, then my mother."

"All right." He started the engine and pulled out of the parking lot. Neither of them spoke. What was there to say?

He found the address of the liquor store and pulled to a stop in front of it. Not a liquor store anymore but a video store. The sandwich shop where Mateo Alvarado's partner, Fred Zamora, had been buying lunch during the shoot-out was half a block away and was now a cellular phone outlet.

"It's conceivable that Zamora didn't see the shooters, except maybe their backs," he said, mentally calculating the distance between the two stores. "By the time the shots registered and he hauled himself out the door—who knows?"

"The employee in the sandwich shop corroborated Zamora's statement," Arianna said.

"But she wasn't out the door as fast as Zamora."

"Are you saying that he saw the shooters, ID'd them but didn't tell anyone?"

"Could be. If this was his patrol area, he could've known them. Maybe he decided not to tell. To deal with it in his own way."

"To avenge my father's murder?"

"I'm thinking out loud. It's one possibility."

"What's another?" she asked.

"I don't know yet."

"You think my mother knows?"

"I think it's unlikely that she doesn't know the case is solved. What else she knows is anyone's guess."

Arianna nodded. "Let's go find out."

Joe admired her ability to focus, to keep her emotions at bay, but he wondered when and how she would deal with the revelations.

Joe wasn't impressed by Hollywood mansions. He'd been in plenty during his career, and he knew that the wealthy and powerful had as many problems as anyone else, if not more. But money bought better attorneys, who made problems go away.

Paloma and Estebán Clemente's home interested him because Arianna grew up there. He pictured her in the Spanish-style house with its tile floors, heavy wood furniture, wrought iron trim, and bold, colorful paintings. The house was cool, elegant and quiet, and scented by huge vases of fresh flowers.

Had the teenage Arianna run barefoot in this house? Played her stereo too loud? Hosted huge, noisy parties for her friends? Hidden a boy in her room for a little necking— or more?

He watched her pace the living room floor, awaiting her mother, who was being summoned by a maid. He hadn't known Arianna long but he knew this mood—all business. She was mentally preparing her list of questions for the interrogation.

Paloma didn't come alone, however. She brought her husband with her. They were a regal looking couple, king and queen of their own principality, this royal mansion. Arianna made the introductions. No one smiled.

"You don't seem surprised to see me, Mom," Arianna said.

"I didn't know when you would come, but I knew you

would." She glanced at Joe. "Someone from the P.D. called to say you'd asked to see Mateo's file."

"Then you were also told I wouldn't be granted access," Joe said.

"I knew if you were anything at all like your father, you would get the information somehow."

"Yes. From my father's personal files."

"Ah. So you know everything."

Arianna took over. "We just came from seeing Mary Beth Maxwell. Horvath, now."

Paloma's eyes glittered, like Arianna's did sometimes, Joe realized. Banked emotion.

Estebán took her hand in his. "She spoke with you?" Paloma asked.

"I think she knew we wouldn't go away until we got some answers. We certainly got answers. And she even apologized for her part in it."

"I'm sorry you found out, *mija*."

Arianna's back stiffened. "Why?"

"Your mother was protecting you," Estebán said. "Surely you can see that. Everyone at the department was protecting you."

"Why would I have to be protected from knowing that my father's killer was dead?"

A curtain of silence dropped over them. Joe's heart began to thud. Even worse, he thought. This was even worse.

Paloma and Estebán exchanged glances. Paloma retreated.

"You said Mary Beth told you everything," Estebán said.

"No. Mom said that. What's everything? What do you think I know?"

"*Mija*—" Paloma bit her lower lip.

"Tell her, Dove," Estebán urged his wife. "It's been a secret too long already."

"As you've said for years," Paloma said wearily.

Joe kept his eyes on Arianna.

"Your father and Mary Beth Maxwell were having an affair at the time he died."

"No!" Arianna jumped up.

Paloma stood more slowly, extending her hands beseechingly toward her daughter. "Yes. I'm sorry, *mija*. It's true. No one wanted you to know. You worshipped him. You wanted to be a cop when you grew up. No one wanted his memory tarnished for you."

"It's not true."

"It's true."

Arianna crossed her arms. "Why the other lie? Why wasn't I told that the case was solved? That the shooter was dead?"

"If they left the case unsolved, no one had access to the files, except those people they chose. We figured eventually no one would remember. The department closed ranks for me—for you. To keep your father good for you."

"Was my father part of that conspiracy?" Joe asked.

"Yes, of course. In fact, it was his idea."

His idea? Joe tried to understand why. Maybe— "Who shot the killer?"

"I can't tell you anything about him."

"You don't know anything about him?" Joe asked, clarifying her ambiguous words.

"Nothing. I was told only that they found him and he was dead. Shot. An eye for an eye."

"Someone said that to you?" Joe pressed.

"No. Maybe. I don't remember. That's how I felt, anyway."

"Yet he was cheating on you." Joe wanted to put his

arms around Arianna, who stood so rigid he thought she might break.

Paloma went stiff. "Mateo and I had our problems, but he was still mine. And he was the father of my daughter. Did I want him avenged? Yes. *Yes.*" She turned to Arianna. "Please sit down, *mija*. We can talk about it."

"It's too late. Let's go," she said to Joe as she stalked past him.

He followed without a goodbye. She flung open the car door and was inside before he reached it. He climbed in, put the key in the ignition, then turned to her.

"Just start the car and go," she said, her jaw hard, her eyes almost black, her lips compressed. "Please. I want to go home."

So he took her home—to his home—prepared to argue if she wanted to go to her apartment. She shouldn't be alone right now. Hell, neither should he. What they'd learned about their fathers in a few short hours was a lifetime's worth of shock.

And undoubtedly there was more to come.

Arianna was grateful that Joe seemed to know when to talk and when not to. As soon as she got to his house she distracted herself by calling Sam and asking if he'd tracked down Fred Zamora yet, which he hadn't. Then she asked her assistant to reschedule her late afternoon appointment. Arianna had no interest in going into the office.

She sank into the living room sofa. Joe joined her there, passing her a bottle of water.

"Too early in the day for a beer?" she asked.

"Up to you."

She twisted the cap off and took a swallow. "No. I don't drown my sorrows."

"What do you do?"

She eyed him as he sat beside her and leaned toward her, his arms resting on his thighs. "Yoga. Or book a one-on-one with my tae kwon do instructor. Or I go running, although that's my least favorite thing to do. Something physical, anyway."

Unlike most men she knew, Joe didn't turn her comment into something sexual. He certainly was different from other men. Quiet, but not someone she could push around. Deliberate, but not one to drag his heels. He knew how to be a partner, too. How to share information. When to let her take the lead. His ego didn't demand he be the one in charge or the center of attention. That was rare.

"My parents fought," she said, opening the discussion.

"Constantly?"

"No. I think it had started shortly before he died—or maybe that's all my memory recalls. They tried to hide it from me, but every once in a while I would wake up at night and hear them, or I would walk into a room and interrupt them. Mom told him to leave once. It couldn't have been too long before the shooting, because I have a vivid picture of the moment." She drank some more water. "Did your parents argue?"

"They would get short with each other, but I can't remember them arguing." He pointed to his bookcase. "See the glass horse-head bookends?"

She nodded. "They were on your parents' bookcase in their living room. I noticed them the day I was there because they were so unusual."

"When one of my parents was mad at the other, he or she would turn the heads to face the other direction."

Arianna smiled. It felt good. "Did that constitute a fight?"

"I guess so. In their world."

"Amazing."

"The time I told you about when my dad was so hard to live with, probably right after your dad was killed, those horses were turned around more than they weren't. But I didn't hear a cross word from either of them." He moved across the room and picked up one of the bookends as if holding it gave him a connection with his parents. "I told my mom once that she and Dad should've argued in front of me. That it was like growing up in Disneyland. When Jane and I had our first argument, I figured the relationship was over."

"How did your mom respond?"

"She said they hadn't intentionally not argued in front of me, that she could count on one hand the number of serious differences of opinion they'd had. They'd gotten good at knowing what mattered to each of them, and who it mattered more to, so the other one would back down."

"That's friendship, as well as love."

He set the horse down, aligned it again with the books. "That's what she said, too. I didn't have that with Jane. I didn't realize it until afterward. It's good that things worked out as they did."

"I can't believe my dad had an affair." There. She'd said the words.

"I can't believe my dad was involved in a cover-up." He sat beside her and took her hand. "It's been a helluva day."

"Yeah."

"Your mom said you worshipped him," Joe said. "That you'd wanted to be a cop."

She squeezed his hand and nodded.

"My dad was high on my list, too," he said. "I can't see him agreeing to a cover-up, much less instigating it."

Arianna heard the pain and shock in his voice. "We don't know that for sure. All we know for sure is that he thought the file should be kept from me. That's not the same thing.''

"True. Does Sam have a lead on Fred Zamora yet?''

"No. He'll find him, Joe.'' They sat in silence for a minute, then she stood. "Let's look at the notes again, knowing what we know now. Something else may jump out at us.''

Late that night when they finally went to bed, she reached for him. He wrapped her in his arms, kissed her hair, then he didn't let go. She fell asleep listening to the steady rhythm of his heart, feeling the comfort of his arms, and knowing he would be there in the morning, strong and steady.

Thirteen

Arianna arrived at her office early the next morning. Only one other car was in the parking lot—Sam's. She went directly to his office, hoping he had information for her.

"You look like hell," he said when he spotted her.

"You're so good for a girl's ego." She sat in a chair opposite his desk. "You don't look so spit and polished yourself."

"Missing my wife. But I'm getting on a plane in a couple of hours for D.C." He leaned back. "What's going on?"

She gave him a rundown of what they'd learned yesterday. He let out a low whistle. "Tough day for both of you. I take it you didn't get much sleep last night."

"Actually, I slept pretty well." Every time she woke up, Joe's arms were still around her. The nightmare didn't surface, maybe because she knew her father's killer was dead. But still there were other questions that needed to be answered before she could put it all to rest. She also had to come to terms with the fact that her father wasn't what he'd seemed to be. And that her mother had lied to her all these years, long after it was necessary to protect Arianna the child.

"Have you moved in with Vicente?" Sam asked.

"Just until we're done finding out what we need to know."

"Enjoying yourself, Ar?"

She found she could smile. "He's...different."

"You can't lead him around by the nose."

For a second she thought she should be offended. However, it's hard to offend with the truth. She liked strong men. She just didn't date them. She didn't like the fight for control that always occurred. "Lovely image, Sam."

"If the nose ring fits..."

She laughed.

He passed her a sheet of paper. "Here's the address on Fred Zamora. Retired a few years ago."

"He lives in San Francisco?"

"Has a daughter there and a couple of grandkids. Will you go up and see him?"

"Definitely."

"Want to meet Doc while you're there and check him out?"

"Sure. He's interested in working for us?"

Sam shrugged. "I wouldn't go that far. But he said he'd talk. Here's his phone number."

"Do we know his real name?"

"Nope. And we probably won't unless we hire him."

"Frankly, I can't imagine him giving up his independence. He gives a whole new meaning to *private* investigator." She stood. "Tell the senator hello for me."

"If we find time to talk, I will."

She smiled as she made her way to her office. When Nate had fallen in love last year, it had changed him a little, settled him in a way Arianna never thought to see him settled. But when Sam fell in love it had opened floodgates. Maybe only someone who knew him as well as she did would see the difference, but they were obvious to Arianna. He smiled more, laughed more, got out in public more. He might not have rivaled Doc for privacy, but he had come close.

She called Joe as soon as she sat at her desk. "I've got an address and phone number for Fred Zamora. He's in San Francisco. Want to fly up there tomorrow?"

"Definitely. We should probably call ahead, though. It's not like we can just drop in and expect him to be home."

She wanted to catch Zamora off guard, as they had Mary Beth Horvath. Arianna glanced at the second sheet of paper that Sam had given her. "Let me work on that. In the meantime I'll get us booked on a flight for early in the morning. Do you like a window or aisle seat?"

"Aisle."

"We have a problem, then, Detective."

"Big surprise. You like aisle, too."

She heard the smile in his voice. She wished she was there, kissing that smile right off his face. She'd deprived herself of a kiss goodbye this morning, just like yesterday. It had seemed too domestic, as if he would expect more of her because of it. "Yes, I like aisle, too," she confirmed.

"We'll flip for it."

She grinned. "A gentleman would give up his seat to a lady."

"What's your point?"

She doodled on a piece of paper. "Maybe I'll get us two aisle seats."

"Suit yourself. By the way, we're going to the movies tonight."

"We are? Why?"

"Because we've been cooped up for too long."

"You mean *you've* been cooped up," she said, but with real sympathy.

"I can't say the rooster has minded being stuck with the chick, but there's more to life than this investigation. Consider this an intervention."

"It's for my own good?"

"And mine."

"Okay."

"Want to know what we'll be seeing?" he asked.

"Surprise me."

"Remember you said that."

After she hung up she looked at what she'd doodled. A heart. A great big heart with an arrow shot through it and the initials A.A. and J.V. She snatched up the sheet and put it down the shredder in the open cabinet behind her, her heart pounding.

It was because he was taking her out on a date, a real date, like in high school, that she'd drawn what she had. A momentary return to adolescence, that was all.

That was all, she repeated to herself, then looked at her watch. How long should she wait to contact Doc? She decided to try him at a more decent hour. She certainly had plenty to keep her busy in the meantime.

The problem was, for the first time since they'd started ARC, she didn't want to be at work. She ignored the stack of paperwork in her in-basket and logged onto the Internet, then she did some research on Alzheimer's disease until the staff began arriving and she had questions to answer and calls to field.

Finally she called Doc. She wondered how old he was

and what he looked like. She needed to remember to ask Sam.

"Good morning. This is Arianna Alvarado from ARC Security & Investigations," she said when he answered.

"Morning."

"Sam says you might be interested in joining our company."

"I might."

"Yes, he stressed that. I find I have to be in San Francisco tomorrow, and I'd like for us to meet, if you've got the time."

"I'll make time."

"Good. I also have a job I could use your help with, if you're interested."

She told him she needed to know if Fred Zamora was at home now, and then again tomorrow morning, so that she and Joe wouldn't waste their trip.

He was silent for several seconds. "You want to pay what I charge for a surveillance assignment that any kid with the ink still fresh on his license could do?"

"That's right."

"It's your money." She could almost hear his shrug. "You'll do it?"

"Sure. What time is your flight?"

"Eight-thirty."

"Give me your cell number. I'll call you in time to cancel your flight if he's not home. If he's home, do you want me to stay there until you arrive? Follow him if he leaves?"

"Yes. Can we meet in the afternoon to talk business?"

"You've got my number."

After Arianna hung up she went to see Sam, who was packing his briefcase, ready to leave for the airport. "Are you sure we should be pursuing this guy, Doc?"

"Yeah, why?"

"You know how important communication skills are with our clients. We've got to be part psychologist. Doc is...brusque."

"I didn't notice that. Maybe he doesn't like women bosses." He grinned.

"Then we definitely don't want him."

"Give him a chance, Ar. Maybe you woke him up or something."

"Okay." She started to leave but turned back. "What's he look like, anyway?"

"Our age, my height and build. Black hair. Looks like he's won a fight or two in his life." He locked his desk drawer. "I'm out of here. I'll be on the red-eye Sunday night. See you Monday morning."

Arianna headed back to her office. She didn't envy him his commuter marriage. But at least he had someone to go home to, even if only on weekends for now.

She stopped just inside her door. Someone to go home to? When had she started envying that?

"Mija?"

Arianna was proud of the fact that she didn't jump at the sound of her mother's voice. She turned around slowly.

"I'm not ready to talk to you yet," Arianna said, crossing her arms.

"I am your mother and you will listen."

Paloma pushed past Arianna and took a seat on the sofa. Not willing to make a scene in front of her staff, Arianna shut the door then leaned against it.

"I am sorry for causing you pain," Paloma said. "It was what I'd been trying to prevent all these years. You must believe me."

"I do—for when I was a child. You could have told me as an adult. And you certainly could've told me two weeks ago when I came to you and said I was going to investigate

on my own. Think of all the trouble you could have prevented."

"I wanted you to keep your faith about your father. No
matter what happened between him and me, he was a good
father. And a good police officer. It was important to me
that you remember him that way."

"He wasn't what he seemed."

"That had nothing to do with you or your relationship
with him. There were things that happened between us that
you don't know about. Things—"

"No!" Arianna came toward her mother. "I don't want
to know, okay? Your marriage is private. I really don't
want to talk about any of this."

"There is one thing you should know." Paloma put her
shoulders back. "Mike Vicente was in love with me."

A hammer against her skull would've had less impact,
Arianna thought, staggered. "I don't believe it."

"I am not bragging. I am ashamed, in fact. But Estebán
convinced me that I needed to tell you the final truth. Now
you know it all."

"I do not believe it." In her head Arianna heard Joe talk
about his parents, about their friendship and love and respect for each other.

"I'm not saying he acted on his feelings for me. He
didn't. And in retrospect I understand that he was drawn to
me—and you, in a way—as strong men are drawn to helpless women. He wanted to take care of us."

"And what did you do?"

"I used that love, or most likely infatuation, to get what
I wanted."

"To get my father's case declared unsolved so that I
wouldn't know he'd been having an affair."

"Yes. And I would do it again."

"How did you end things with Mr. Vicente?"

"Gently. Will you tell his son?"

"I don't see how I can't. What's one more disappoint-ment? Might as well get them all over with."

Paloma closed her eyes for a few seconds. "We're all human, *mija*. It was a horrible time in my life. I am not proud of how I dealt with your father, nor of how I tempted Mike with promises of more. I have tried to make amends by living a charitable life since then. I made a mistake, a big one, but I learned from it. Everyone deserves a second chance."

Maybe. In time, Arianna thought. In time. "I can't talk to you any more, Mom."

Her mother stood. She gripped Arianna's shoulders. *"Te amo, mija."*

"I love you, too. I just need to figure out what I'm feel-ing now."

"All right." She left the room, her scent lingering.

Arianna couldn't stand to be there a moment longer. Joe. She wanted to see Joe. She had to tell him. God. What else were they going to learn? How many more earth-shattering revelations were ahead? Would Fred Zamora have a few?

She grabbed her purse and headed for the front door, then detoured to Nate's office.

"Hey," she said from his doorway.

He looked up, started to speak but rose instead and came to her. He tugged on her arm until she was inside the door, which he shut behind her.

He held her by her shoulders. "What's going on, Ar?" he asked.

"Too much to explain right now. I just wanted to let you know that I'm taking the day off. Can you field the calls?"

"Sure." He released her. "I don't think I've seen that look on your face since we thought we were going to die."

"I haven't felt this way since then." Hollow and scared.

"Is it Vicente? Is he giving you grief?"

"No. I'm about to give him some, and I hate the thought of doing it." She drew a deep breath. "I'll see you later."

"I'll be around all weekend if you need me."

"Okay. Thanks."

Arianna rolled all the windows down in the car before she headed out of the parking lot. Her hair blew wildly, her skin chilled. She tried to let her mind go blank. Soon she was passing the house where Joe's father lived. She saw Joe's car out front and pulled up behind it. Almost blindly she walked up to the front door and knocked. A middle-aged woman answered. Her eyes were kind.

"Hi," Arianna said. "I'm here to see Mike Vicente. I see Joe's car out front. Would you let him know Arianna is here, please."

"You can just go back. Do you know where his room is?"

"Yes. Are you sure?" she asked, worried about surprising them.

"I'm sure." She smiled. "Mike loves company."

Arianna almost tiptoed down the hall. The door to Mike's room was open. She could hear Joe talking.

"I'll only be gone one day, Dad. I'll bring you a loaf of sourdough. Would you like that?"

She didn't hear an answer.

"You took me to San Francisco when I was sixteen. We went to watch the Dodgers play the Giants the final game of the season. I've never forgotten that. The Dodgers won in the twelfth inning."

Arianna stepped into the doorway. Joe was massaging lotion into his father's feet. His tender touch broke her heart. His gentle smile for his father made her eyes sting.

How could she tell him his father had been in love with another woman? How could she?

She couldn't, she realized. Did he really need to know? What would it accomplish? Nothing except cause unnecessary pain to a man already burdened with enough.

Chief spotted her. His tail thumped in greeting.

"There you are," Mike said.

Joe turned his head. His eyes lit up.

Don't look at me like that, Joe, she thought.

Do look at me like that.

Her stomach swirled then settled. Her heart calmed. She smiled and stepped into the room. "Yes, here I am."

Fourteen

―――

Joe scouted a parking spot while Arianna used her cell phone to call Doc when they got to their destination. Their flight to San Francisco was uneventful. She'd even taken the window seat, with no fuss about it—which worried him. He would have given up the aisle seat after he'd teased her about it a little.

"It's Arianna," he heard her say into the phone. "We're in Zamora's neighborhood. Driving a blue Taurus. Do you see us?... Good. Is he still at home?... Great. What?... Okay, thanks. I'll call you when we're done here."

Arianna pointed to an almost unnoticeable gray sedan pulling out. "We can take his parking spot."

She'd been unusually quiet since she'd surprised him at his dad's facility yesterday. Even the movie, a Western he thought would completely distract her, hadn't roused any discussion. He questioned her about it but she shrugged it off. Still reeling from everything they'd learned, she told him. Then she made love to him with a passion that felt almost desperate.

She amazed him. Fascinated him. Even when she tried to put a barrier between them, like not kissing him goodbye or hello, she intrigued him, because he wondered what her reasoning was. So many layers. Such a complicated woman. Tender and tough. Sweet and strong. She would never bore.

"I wonder what surprise we're in for this time," she said, grabbing the door handle.

"Let's hope he answers the rest of our questions."

"Careful what you wish for," she said, then climbed out of the car.

Fred Zamora lived on the first floor of a two-story four-plex in an old San Francisco neighborhood, half a block away from his daughter and her family. The neighborhood teemed with Saturday morning activity. Walkers and joggers, with dogs and without. People shuffling home with grocery bags. Car exhaust got taken away in the same ocean breeze as the fog, the day promising to be clear and crisp. Autumn at its most beautiful, and so different from Southern California.

Joe noted Arianna's tension, but he doubted it was any greater than his.

She rang the bell. A few seconds later the door was opened by a man in his early sixties, with gunmetal gray hair and wary eyes. His belly hung over his belt.

"Mr. Zamora?" Arianna said.

"Yeah."

"I'm Arianna Alvarado."

He clenched the door, but he schooled his face quickly. "Anyone tell you that you look a bit like your mother?"

"Sometimes. This is Joe Vicente."

"Mike's kid?"

Joe nodded as he extended his hand.

To Arianna, Fred said, "Been wondering when you would turn up. Heard you were a P.I. A good one. Figured you'd be asking questions one of these days. Come on in."

The apartment was unremarkable. According to the file Sam put together, Fred had been divorced—his second—for many years, and the lack of a woman's touch was evident. Functional furniture and few accessories. Joe wondered how he spent his time. Did he work? Hang out at a bar?

Fred sat in what was obviously his television chair, as it was aimed at the screen and held a deep indentation from his body.

"How's your mother?" he asked Arianna.

"She's well, thank you."

"That was some second marriage she managed."

Arianna didn't respond. Joe heard resentment in his voice and wondered about it.

"I'd like to talk about my father," she said.

"Shoot."

"Would you tell me what happened that day?"

He crossed his arms. "We stopped for lunch. I went to get us sandwiches, and coffee for me. He was getting cigarettes and a soft drink. I heard shots. I put my head out the door but I didn't see anyone."

"Not even people on the street?" Joe asked. It still seemed incredible that at noon in that neighborhood no one was out walking.

"A few cars," Fred said with a shrug. "I wasn't sure where the shots came from, but Mateo didn't come out of the liquor store, which didn't seem right, so I headed there. I found him, already dead, and the clerk, shot up bad."

"Was that your patrol area?" Joe asked.

Fred looked from Joe to Arianna, hesitance in his eyes.

"I already know my father was having an affair with the clerk," she said.

He heaved a sigh. "The store was out of our zone, but we weren't breaking any rules. You could leave the area when you were out of service, like for lunch."

"Did you go there often?" Arianna asked.

"Yeah."

"For how long?"

"Ten, maybe fifteen minutes."

"I mean," she said, "how long had my father been seeing her?"

"Oh. I don't remember exactly. A few weeks."

"You approved?" Joe asked.

"Hell, no. My first wife divorced me because I cheated. I kept telling him it wasn't worth it. But he was my partner."

Joe understood that. Partners stood up for each other. Covered each other. Sometimes lied for each other.

"What'd you do when you got on scene?" Joe asked.

"Determined that Mateo was beyond my help, then kept pressure on the woman's wounds until the medics could take over. A whole lot of patrol units got there in a hurry and combed the neighborhood. No one knew anything about the shooting or the possible shooters."

He was too calm, Joe thought. He would've been panicking at Mateo's condition. He made it sound like Mateo was any other victim, which wasn't true. "Or they knew something but weren't talking," Joe said.

"I always figured as much. Except it was a cop who was shot. We could usually get someone to break down and tell, one way or another. Snitches in every neighborhood."

"Except this one, apparently."

Fred shrugged again. "Apparently."

"My father's service revolver was missing."

"I noticed that right off."

"Got any ideas about that?" Joe asked.

"I figured the shooters grabbed it."

"Why would they take the time to do that?"

"Free gun. A better one than the Saturday Night Specials they were using."

"I would think they'd want to get out of there in a hurry."

"You asked. I'm speculating. What else could've happened?"

"You could've taken it," Joe said.

Fred slouched in his chair and steepled his fingers in front of his face. "Why would I do that?"

"Good question."

Arianna leaned forward. "Do you know how it happened to turn up in Joe's father's possession?"

Joe didn't react to her lie. If she could get more information out of Zamora by fudging the truth about knowing who that weapon belonged to, Joe wasn't going to split hairs over it.

"That would be a question for Mike," Fred said, looking at Joe.

"My father has Alzheimer's."

"Oh, yeah. I'd heard that. I'm real sorry." He sat a little taller. "Look, why are you pushing this? The guy who killed your father is dead. Justice was served. What more do you want?"

"I didn't know until day before yesterday that justice had been served," Arianna said. "I have a need to know what happened."

"Open and shut. You already know the details."

"No. If that was all there was to it, I would've been told before now."

Joe hadn't thought about it like that. She was right, though. So what was missing?

"My theory," Fred said, "is that some pal of the shooter had a beef with him and shot him with the gun stolen from your father."

"How would it end up in Mike Vicente's possession?"

"Are you sure it's Mateo's gun?"

"Yes."

Joe watched her state the bald-faced lie, knowing what she was after. If Fred knew that the serial number on the gun in his dad's safe had been filed off, he also knew they couldn't positively identify the weapon as Mateo's—and that Arianna was bluffing. In fact, if Fred mentioned the serial number at all, he implicated himself.

And Joe's father.

"You positively ID'd it?" was all Fred asked.

"We did," Arianna said.

"I don't have an answer for that."

"Liar." Arianna's jaw clenched. "You know. You're just not telling."

"What does it matter? Really? What does it matter? Nothing changes."

"I think you saw the killer at the scene," she said. "I think you knew who he was and didn't tell anyone. I think you took my father's gun yourself and sought out the killer and shot him yourself."

"If I'd shot the guy, I would've used a weapon that the P.D. didn't already have a ballistics report on."

Arianna stood. "We're wasting our time." She headed out of the room.

Joe followed.

"Wait," Fred said, loud enough to stop her. He ambled up to her. "I loved Mateo like a brother. He was a good cop and a good guy. Always bragging about you. Saved my butt a couple of times. You heard the saying about letting sleeping dogs lie? You need to do that. Nothing you find out can bring him back.'' He looked at Joe. ''Convince her.''

''I'm looking for answers, too. And my father is still alive.''

''Let sleeping dogs lie.''

Arianna yanked open the front door. It was as much anger as he'd seen her display since they'd met.

''Well, that was a complete waste of time,'' she said once they were in the car.

''Not entirely.''

''What do you mean?''

''I mean it's apparent there's a conspiracy of some kind.''

''A conspiracy of silence,'' she said, crossing her arms.

''Maybe he has a point, Arianna. Maybe we should give it up.'' *Maybe I don't want to know how my father was involved in this.*

''Not yet.''

''If you find out that Zamora did the killing, would you turn him in?'' he asked.

''I don't know. Would you?'' Her eyes looked bleak.

He didn't answer.

''You're a cop,'' she said. ''You uphold the law.''

''What I think about this case doesn't matter. No D.A. would want it. No cop would want to deal with it. Not twenty-five years after the fact. Not for a cop killer.''

She was quiet for a moment, then, ''You really think I should stop looking?''

''I won't tell you what to do,'' he said. It would be useless to try, anyway.

''And you would be content not knowing your father's part in it?''

"Content isn't the word I would use, but I would be willing to let it go. Dad can't tell us anything, and he can't be punished."

After a minute she pulled out her cell phone and dialed. "It's Arianna. We're done. Where can we meet you?"

Joe waited until she'd written down the directions Doc gave her for where to meet, then he leaned across the console and gave her a hug. She resisted for a few seconds, then she buried her face against his neck and let out a long, shaky breath.

"That was a bad interrogation," she said, relaxing against him.

"He's a pro. You couldn't have broken him no matter what you said. You did fine."

She pulled away. He brushed her hair back, glad he had come with her, even though she would've managed fine without him. Her honesty was refreshing, her intelligence a magnet that pulled him in, her passion more than a little addictive. He knew it wasn't to his benefit to tell her to give up the inquiry, since she would probably move back to her apartment when they were done, but he couldn't keep her with a lie. For her sake he thought she should give it up. What was done was done.

"Let's go meet Doc," she said.

"I'll drop you off then come back and get you."

"You can stay. I'd like your opinion, too. If you don't mind."

"You don't think it'll bother him?"

"I doubt very much he's going to come work for us. He's a lone wolf, that's for sure. So, you might as well meet him, too. This will be as casual a job interview as I've ever conducted."

He pulled away from the curb and turned left at the first

stop sign, following her directions. "If you don't think he's the right person for the job, why are you bothering?"

"Because we need someone in San Francisco, preferably three someones. Doc's not only good, he brings a client list, and I gather it's the kind of client we usually deal with, not just skip traces or spousal infidelities. I think his rates are higher than ours."

He gave the car some gas to climb one of San Francisco's famous hilly streets and enjoyed the ride. "So he doesn't need you, but you need him. That puts him in the driver's seat."

"It sure does."

He pictured a face-off between Arianna and Doc. "This ought to be entertaining," he said, smiling at her, then glad to see her smile in return.

"You can keep score."

"Or referee. Too bad I left my black-and-white striped shirt at home."

She laughed, and he relaxed at last.

Arianna let her eyes adjust to the dark interior of the charming Italian restaurant. Soon she saw a lone man at a table near the kitchen, his back to the wall. That wouldn't make Joe happy, she thought. Cops always wanted to sit with their backs to the wall and facing the room. She did, too.

She walked to the table, feeling Joe's presence behind her.

"Doc?" she said.

He stood, shook hands with them, then settled into his seat. "I waited for you to order."

He had light brown eyes with more than a hint of gold, Arianna noticed. Olive skin, black hair, not really handsome but appealing in a rough-around-the-edges way.

She realized he was waiting for her to speak. "I'm not really hungry."

"I am," Joe said, picking up a menu. "What do you recommend?"

"The artichoke ravioli," Doc said. "Or spaghetti and meatballs. The best in the city."

Arianna decided it would be rude not to eat, so she ordered angel hair pasta with basil and fresh tomatoes.

"You get what you needed from Zamora?" Doc asked.

"We got what he would give us," Arianna said. "Which wasn't much. I appreciate your keeping an eye on him for us."

"You'll get my bill."

"I'm sure. Look, are you interested in the least in coming to work for ARC or am I just spinning my wheels here?"

"Direct. I like that. Well, Ms. Alvarado, if I weren't 'interested in the least' I wouldn't be here."

Arianna waited until their server put their iced teas on the table before she continued. "I think Sam told you we want to open a branch office in the city. He wants you."

"You say that as if you don't."

"I have a hard time trusting someone who doesn't give his name."

"You're wondering what I'm hiding?"

"Yes."

He stirred some sugar into his tea, keeping her waiting, his expression benign. She wanted to dislike him, but she found she couldn't. He seemed amused by her, but not in a condescending way.

"I wonder if you know what your reputation is," he said.

"It's solid. We worked hard to earn it."

"I mean you personally."

She glanced at Joe in time to see the hint of a smile on

his lips. She leaned back, crossed her legs and lifted her brows. "You're going to tell me, I assume."

"Smart," Doc said. "The logic skills of a man. Not afraid to use your body as a weapon, physically and sexually."

"I don't prostitute to get information."

"Didn't mean it that way. I meant you're not opposed to using your cleavage as a distraction. Some men are stupid enough to fall for that."

Joe laughed. Choked. Took a swallow of tea. Over the rim of his glass he met Arianna's steely gaze.

Doc eyed Joe. "Who are you, exactly? I haven't seen your name as part of the firm."

"LAPD. Robbery-Homicide division."

Doc raised his glass in a toast. "Last I checked, cops and P.I.s don't exactly collaborate."

"We're proving it's a myth," Arianna said, realizing she wasn't offended by his description of her. It was the truth, after all. Although the "logic skills of a man" part could've been considered an insult. "Joe and I partnered up on an investigation. A personal one."

Over lunch Arianna and Joe shared the details of the case. Doc asked good questions then, as they finished, he said, "I'd look at the woman again."

"Mary Beth?" Arianna asked.

"Both of you thought there was something off with her."

"Yes, but then we found out it was because she was having an affair with my father."

"Maybe that's not all there was to it. Your mother said she told you everything she knew. Zamora won't tell you anything else. Joe's father's notes might not ever be deciphered. Mary Beth is the only one left."

"We'll talk it over. So—" she set her silverware on her

empty plate "—are you ready to work out of an office? Have people know your name? Come out of the shadows and into the light?"

He actually smiled. "Maybe. I'll let you know."

"We offer great benefits. A steady income. Bonuses."

"We'd have to talk about money. I'm not taking a cut. In fact, I figure you'd owe me a signing bonus for what I'd be bringing to your firm."

"Everything's negotiable."

"All right. I'll get back to you."

When? she wanted to ask, but knew she couldn't push him. Actually, he was a lot like Sam, which is probably why she liked him right away. "You've got my number," she said.

He nodded then stood. "I'll be interested in knowing how your personal case comes out."

"I'm only sharing that with ARC employees," she said sweetly.

He laughed and shook her hand.

"Not averse to female bosses, are you, Doc?" she asked.

"Averse to bosses in general, Arianna. But I could probably work with you okay. See you." He included Joe in his farewells then was gone.

"That was entertaining," Joe said.

Arianna felt better than she had in days. "Yes, it was."

"Do you think he'll work for you?"

"If we can meet his demands, yes."

"Will you meet them?"

"We'd be crazy not to."

He folded his napkin and set it beside his plate. "So, if I were interested in working for ARC, would you hire me?"

His tone was casual, but his expression wasn't. "You've

got what it takes,'' she said. ''But I think you like being a cop too much to leave.''

''That wasn't my question.''

''Would I hire you? I'd be crazy not to.'' She stood, ending the discussion. The thought of them working together was way too appealing. ''Let's go home.''

Fifteen

On Sunday morning Joe set down rules for the day—all play, no work. They couldn't go to see Mary Beth Horvath until Monday, anyway, but he also wanted a day without examining, discussing and agonizing over their fathers. Just one day. By tomorrow the investigation would probably have run its course. Either they'd have the truth or they'd have to learn to live with never knowing the truth.

So, today was critical. Arianna was becoming as obsessed as he'd been when he was dealing with his parents' illnesses, his broken engagement, then his mother's death and a case he couldn't solve, no matter how hard he tried. He didn't want Arianna to reach the point of burnout that he had. She needed to find the balance he'd only recently found again himself.

"A day of play," she said as they sipped coffee and read the Sunday paper in his bed. "What will we do?"

He smiled at her look of bewilderment. "You say that like you have no idea what a day off means."

"I know what it means. I just don't do it much. Not an entire day."

She looked beautiful, as she always did first thing in the morning, without makeup, her hair mussed, and wearing one of his shirts.

"We go out someplace nice for brunch," he said. "We see if the Jackie Chan marathon you missed last week is still running. Or we drive down to San Diego and go to the zoo or Sea World. We play, Arianna. We have fun."

She set her coffee mug on the nightstand then faced him, sitting cross-legged. "You have tickets to a Lakers game. I saw them tucked into your bedroom mirror the first night I was here. You took them down, but I saw they were for today."

He folded up the sports section and slipped it under the classified ads. "Four of us went in on two season tickets years ago."

"So you go to every fourth game?"

"It doesn't work out that neatly, but that's the theory."

"Did you give your tickets for today away?"

She was in an interrogation mode. Her gaze never wavered. Her tone of voice was matter-of-fact. He knew exactly where her line of questioning was headed.

"I haven't given the tickets away yet, but I won't have any problem finding someone who wants them," he said then leaned against the headboard and waited.

"I'd like to go."

No surprise there. "Why?"

"I've never been to a game."

"Do you follow basketball?"

"I read the sports section. I know the players' names. Why weren't you going to tell me about the tickets?" She didn't pause long enough to let him answer. "Do you see Jane there?"

Finally, the question he'd been waiting for. "Occasionally. It's her job to be there. But we haven't spoken." He had nothing to say to his former fiancée.

"Have you taken dates to games before?"

"Yes."

Something flickered in her eyes. Jealousy? It was hard to believe. She would be the one to make other women jealous.

"But not this season, which has barely started. I've only taken a buddy," he said, intrigued by her businesslike demeanor. She'd told him once that she'd never even considered marriage. Did she hold men at bay by keeping control of her feelings as well as the relationship? He could see how that could easily happen, except she had yielded to him at times during the past couple of weeks, so maybe he was off-base about that. "Do you really want to go?"

"I do."

He liked that she didn't play any games with him. She didn't act coy, but was direct. "Okay."

"There's time for brunch first, though, right?"

He managed to get her flat on the mattress and under him with a couple of quick maneuvers. She had the expertise to have prevented him from gaining dominance, so he took it as acceptance that she was in the position she was in.

"We have time for lots of things first," he said.

She looped her arms around his neck, pulling him down for a kiss. "A marathon?"

"Tonight," he said against her lips. It would probably be their last night together in his house. He would give her a reason to come back—provided what they learned about their fathers wasn't too much for them to overcome.

* * *

Joe watched Arianna disappear into the crowd at Staples Center, home of the L.A. Lakers. Knowing how long the line was for the women's restroom, he leaned his shoulders against a nearby wall and got comfortable, a boot propped against the wall and a beer in hand.

He'd enjoyed watching her not only take in the game but become a part of it. She shouted every sports cliché known to man, making particular reference to one referee's apparent visual and intellectual handicaps, then she looked at Joe and grinned, her eyes sparkling.

He'd been wrong. She knew how to have fun.

"Joe?"

He turned toward the voice, but he already knew who it was. Jane. She looked different. She'd cut her blond hair short and wasn't wearing her glasses. She wore a Lakers-purple pantsuit on her petite body. He towered over her, a thought that confused him. She hadn't seemed short when he'd been with her.

He wondered at his lack of reaction to seeing her now. Nothing. He felt nothing.

"Enjoying the game?" she asked.

"Too close for comfort."

She smiled. "They'll come back in the second half. How have you been?"

He hoped Arianna would be delayed a while longer. Introducing her to Jane would likely take the fun out of the play day. "I'm well. You?"

"I'm fine, thanks. I see you brought a date."

Yeah, so? he wanted to say. Instead he said nothing.

"You look happy, Joe."

"I am." He hadn't realized how happy until she pointed it out. At some point during the week his insomnia had disappeared and his stomach settled down to banked coals instead of a roaring fire. He could remember his mother as she was before the cancer. And his father before the Alzheimer's had claimed his mind. Joe was feeling very good about all of it.

"So, you're over us," she said.

"Long ago."

She winced a little at that. "Good. I wouldn't have made you happy, you know. Not for long. I was naive about what it's like being married to a cop. I thought loving you would be enough. But your mother set me straight about that."

He came to attention. "My mother? When was that?"

She frowned. "I told you before. During her first round of chemo, when I took her to her doctor's appointment."

"I don't remember."

"I asked her how she dealt with a man who wouldn't share his feelings."

"I remember you saying that, but I thought you were talking about my father."

"Why would I care about that?"

He didn't know, but she hadn't told him the question had been about him. "What did she say?"

"That I would learn not to take it personally. That men, especially cops, think they're doing women a favor by not sharing what they see on the job and how they react to it. I knew I couldn't live with a man who didn't share the bad along with the good."

He realized then why he'd loved her once. She'd tried to get him to open up. She'd tried hard.

She laid a hand on his arm. He couldn't pull away without making it seem too important.

"I left something out when I told you about that talk with your mom," she said, her voice hushed. "She said that no matter what I did or how hard I tried, sometimes I wouldn't be able to reach you. And that sometimes if I tried too hard, it would have the opposite effect, and you would

go to someone else, someone uncomplicated and unde-
manding.''

Her words stunned him, especially since they'd come
from his mother. ''Meaning I would cheat?''

''Only that the possibility existed. I realized I didn't want
to live with that or deal with that.''

''I would say that possibility exists in every relationship,
not just a cop's.''

''True. But I'd seen the truth already. You took care of
your parents—you alone. You hardly ever let me help. You
thought I couldn't handle it.''

''You couldn't. You told me it was too much for you.''

''I meant the way you shut down and shut me out.'' She
dropped her hand from his arm. ''Look, Joe, I'm sorry. I
don't know why I brought it up. It's over and done.'' She
turned away.

The meaning behind her words finally sank in. He
grabbed her arm. ''Are you saying my father had an affair?''

''Your mother didn't say so specifically.''

Added to the possibility his father had been part of a
cover-up over Mateo Alvarado's murder, the idea that he'd
cheated on his mother numbed Joe. Impossible. His parents
had been best friends as well as partners. Jane had misun-
derstood his mother, that's all. She'd been speaking in gen-
eralities.

''I really am sorry, Joe. I only meant to say hello and
that I'm glad you're happy again.'' She walked away.

He didn't watch her. He didn't see anything until Arianna put herself directly in front of him.

''What's wrong?'' she asked, concern in her eyes.

''Nothing,'' he said after a moment. ''Nothing.'' He
flung an arm around her shoulders and headed back to their

seats, realizing he was doing exactly what Jane said. He wasn't sharing his feelings.

But this wasn't the time or place for this particular disclosure. Maybe later. After they finished their investigation and there was no reason for her to stay at his house any longer. Maybe then.

Maybe.

Arianna sat on the bench beside the koi pond in Joe's backyard that evening while Joe returned a couple of phone calls. She'd waited all afternoon for him to tell her he'd talked with his former fiancée, but he hadn't brought it up. Not that Arianna knew for sure, but the conversation she'd observed between Joe and the blonde was too intense to be anything superficial. Arianna had hung back so that they wouldn't see her, so they could deal with whatever serious business was there between them, but also because she hadn't wanted to be introduced to the woman who'd broken Joe's heart.

Compounded by a difficult visit with Joe's father before the game, when Mike had been more confused than Joe recalled seeing him, Arianna was ready for the marathon he'd promised. More than ready. Eager. Anxious. She wanted him to forget about Jane and whatever that woman had said to put the look of shock Arianna had seen on his face. She wanted him to forget everything tonight except pleasure.

"Nice evening," Joe said, joining her on the bench by straddling it, wrapping his arms around her waist and pulling her against his chest.

"Beautiful." She rested her arms on his and closed her eyes.

"All day," he said close to her ear, "I've been intrigued

by this tiny bit of black lace.'' He hooked a finger into the
V of her blouse and exposed more than a bit of her bra.

"Good," she said, smiling.

"Tease."

"You promised me a marathon. You don't think that was
the ultimate tease?"

"You've been thinking about it?" he asked.

"Only every second." She felt him unbutton her blouse,
not hurrying, then with his thumb and forefinger he rubbed
the teardrop-shaped gold pendant that lay just above her
cleavage. He slipped his little finger under the edge of her
bra and followed the line down to the clasp then up the
other side. She let out a shaky breath.

She tried to turn around. He wouldn't let her.

"Relax," he whispered into her ear.

She laughed, a small, quavering burst of air. "Then don't
keep doing what you're doing."

"Oh, I fully intend to keep doing it. But you need to
relax and enjoy it."

He stripped her blouse off her and set it across the bench
in front of her. "Better?" he asked.

She nodded. "It would be even better if you took off
your shirt."

He stripped it off and tossed it on top of her blouse, then
he nestled her against him again, skin to skin. She kicked
off her shoes. Her skirt had shifted high on her thighs. He
grabbed the fabric and tugged it even higher, until her legs
were exposed to the night air.

He ran his hands along her thighs. "These are classified
as weapons, aren't they? I like it when you wrap them
around me and squeeze tight. I feel locked in."

He dipped his fingers under her skirt, ran his fingertips
lightly over her panties. She lifted toward his hand but he
only toyed with her.

"You're driving me crazy," she said, feeling out of control and yet not wanting to have any control, either. She wanted to get lost in his arms.

"Crazy's good."

"I'll remind you that you said that."

Joe wanted to dominate. He wanted not just to share the experience but to overwhelm her, to take her places she hadn't been, higher and deeper, and keep her there for longer than she'd ever experienced or ever would again.

Her bra clasp gave him little trouble. Soon his hands were filled with her breasts. He needed those hard nipples in his mouth right now.

"Stand up," he whispered urgently.

She didn't hesitate but stood on the bench, facing him. He reached around her, unzipped her skirt and let it slide to the bench. She kicked it aside and waited.

He ignored the ache in his loins that was demanding satisfaction, pulled her down to straddle his lap, finally tasting her breasts, ignoring her nipples until she guided his head and held him tight, begging him.

The begging was nice, inspiring him to drag everything out longer. He figured she didn't beg often. When he had his fill of her, he laid her down on the bench. She gasped at the initial touch of cold wood against her back then seemed to forget it as he slipped her panties off.

"Joe," she said, her voice full of need.

"Relax."

She laughed, a strangled sound, flattering him. He dragged his fingers down her body lightly again and again. Finally he indulged himself and let his fingertips drift between her thighs. One thing he'd learned—a light touch beat out a heavy one any day.

He explored her gently, keeping a slow, steady pace, deepening a touch when she made a needy sound, moving on when the sound turned to one indicating imminent satisfaction. Not yet, Arianna. Not yet.

He put his mouth on her and she went still, only a long, low moan coming from her. Then she moved, up toward him, enough to let him slide a finger inside her. She lurched higher. He lifted his head.

"Don't...stop," she said, urgent and demanding, trying to pull him back.

But he was afraid she would make too much noise and his neighbors might hear. He slid off the bench, removed the rest of his clothes then sat again, pulling her onto his lap.

"You're going to be the death of me," she murmured against his mouth.

"What a way to go."

He felt her lips form a smile before her tongue got into the game. He held her head in place, keeping her mouth covered as he lifted her, then brought her down on him. Her mouth opened. He pulled her back, stopping the threatening sound with his own mouth.

She angled away. "Good," she whispered. "This is so good."

She moved against him, her nipples brushing his chest, her belly gliding along his. She felt glorious. Tight and wet and slick. He squeezed his eyes shut, tried not to think about how she was the most dazzling woman he'd ever met and that, even after more than a week with her, he could hardly believe he was making love with her now. He felt her clench inside, around him, her tempo increasing to an urgent level. As she burst into a climax he grabbed her head and pulled her mouth to his, swallowing the sounds.

The wooden bench cut into his legs, distracting him, for which he was grateful, but making him even more aware of her.

"Aren't you going to join me?" she asked, her movements slowing.

"In a minute. In the house. I don't want anyone to overhear."

He took her by the hand. Watching her walk naked beside him would rank at the top of his memories. The way her body moved, her confidence, the need he still saw in her eyes—all of it registered.

In his bedroom he jerked back the covers. They could have freedom here.

He followed her down onto the bed. She reached for him.

"I'm not done yet," he said, grabbing her wrist, stopping her.

"I don't know whether to be terrified or thrilled."

He noted the lack of terror in her eyes. "You can let me know later."

"I'll do that."

He kissed her, a long, searching, searing kiss that built then lingered then swelled again. He touched her, the freedom almost painful. He tasted her, a feast he would never forget. She was everything he'd dreamed of and nothing like he'd dreamed. She finally stopped trying to take control, to please *him*, but gave herself up to it—to him. It satisfied him enormously. Eventually he let her reach the top, then after a while, rise above it. She didn't scream exactly, but she would've been loud enough in the yard to have the neighbors wondering.

He didn't let her come down all the way but plunged into her, then stopped. She rose to meet him. He moved slowly, methodically. She tried to increase the pace. He resisted. He had no idea where his ability to resist came from. Some soul-deep need to cherish her as no one had, to plant in her a memory she could pluck from the air now and then and think of him. He didn't want her to forget.

But finally even he had to acknowledge the need and purpose and let himself find oblivion. He almost didn't last long enough to bring her to climax again, but he did, then he followed with an explosion that lasted for hours or days or months. An eternity, at least. Then he woke up on the other side of heaven with her still in his arms, not a dream, after all, not even elusive, but real and warm and all woman.

"You are a generous man," she said quietly, shifting a little.

He moved aside, taking his weight off her, but not losing contact. "No. Completely selfish."

"You need to check your dictionary."

"This is just the beginning," he said, nuzzling her neck.

She arched her back and sighed. "I'll take over for Heartbreak Hill, Marathon Man. See if you can make it over the rise."

He grinned leisurely. "Here. I'll pass you the baton."

Sixteen

The next morning, the front door to Mary Beth Horvath's house opened before Arianna or Joe had a chance to knock.

"I figured you would be back," Mary Beth said, inviting them in as if resigned to the ordeal. "Thank you for waiting until my family was gone."

"If there was more to say, why didn't you just tell us before?" Arianna asked, taking a seat on the same sofa as before, glad that Joe was beside her.

"I was hoping I wouldn't have to. I should've known better. Mike Vicente's son and Mateo's daughter? You wouldn't quit until you had all your answers."

"Did you love my father?" Arianna asked, surprising herself. It wasn't the first question she'd had on her mental list. She felt Joe react to it, too, felt the heat from his body as he moved a little closer. In comfort? Or to remind her to stick to the facts of the case?

"Yes," Mary Beth answered, apology in her eyes.

"How did you meet?"

"He and his partner got me away from my boyfriend before he beat me to death. Your dad came to the hospital after to make sure I wasn't going back to Rollie, my boyfriend." She shook her head. "I don't know how it happened with Mateo. He was just being nice. He helped me find a new job and a place to live. He'd come by the store every day I was working to see that I was okay and that Rollie hadn't tracked me down after he'd been let out of jail. Mateo was like my knight in shining armor, and I just kept falling for him…. He talked about you a lot."

Arianna realized she didn't want or need the details of her father's affair.

"Tell us what happened the day of the murder," Joe said, somehow picking up on her feelings.

Mary Beth's shoulders drooped, as if settled to her fate. "Mateo came into the store at lunchtime, as usual. A few seconds later Rollie and a friend came in, but I didn't see them because I was crouched under the counter opening a new carton of cigarettes to get Mateo a pack. When I stood up I saw Rollie. He'd pulled a gun on Mateo. The friend had one trained on me. Rollie took your dad's gun, then he shot him with it. Just like that. Shot him. Point blank. Then he shot me."

"With his own .22," Joe said.

"I didn't know that at the time. I just knew I'd been shot and left for dead. Mateo's partner…"

"Fred Zamora," Arianna said.

"Yes. He came running through the door right after they left. Then I was unconscious until a couple of days later in the hospital."

"So, Fred saw the shooters."

She nodded.

"And recognized one as your ex-boyfriend, because he and Mateo had broken up a fight between you before."

"Yes. He came to the hospital after I regained consciousness and told me I needed to say I barely knew Mateo, that he was a cop who came to the store every so often, but that was all. That it needed to look like a robbery. He told me to say I couldn't remember anything, that way no one could challenge me about it."

"Did he tell you why?" Joe asked.

"Because if Mateo was shot in the line of duty, not a love triangle, his widow wouldn't have the public humiliation of our affair. Fred said I owed Mateo that much. And you," she said to Arianna. "I owed it to you. I knew that. He loved you so much."

Arianna's stomach twisted. It made her sick to think of her father talking about her with the woman he was sleeping with. *I didn't know you at all, did I, Dad?*

"Then my father discovered the truth," Joe said.

"At some point. I don't know when."

"He would've learned about the fight Mateo and Fred broke up between you and Rollie just by running your name in the computer. He would've known that they were the responding officers," Joe said. "Made the connection. Known Rollie was a potential suspect."

"I suppose. Your father came to me after a couple of weeks, just when I got out of the hospital, and said they got the killer."

"They?"

"I don't know who he meant."

"Then how did he know who the killer was if neither you nor Fred Zamora identified him?"

"I never asked for the name, and he never told me. But he looked at me like he knew I'd been holding back. Then he walked out. I never saw him again. And Rollie disappeared.'' She closed her eyes, exhaustion lining her face. ''That's all I can tell you. Honest. There's nothing more.'' She pushed herself up from the chair. ''Please go now. And please don't ever come back. I've paid for what happened, in ways you don't know. I will pay until the day I die.''

Arianna headed for the door. Mary Beth was right. There was nothing left to say.

In Joe's car a few minutes later tension thickened the air, hot and heavy. She waited for him to start the conversation, but he didn't. He gripped the steering wheel. His jaw clenched and unclenched, clenched and unclenched. She swallowed against the ache in her throat. Was she better off knowing what she knew now? Would ignorance be better? It would be easier, of course, but better? She needed time to let everything sink in before she could answer that question.

Their silence continued as they entered Joe's house. He went directly into the dining room and started boxing up all the paperwork pertaining to the case—his father's notes and his own. She stacked hers, intending to take them with her.

Should she gather her personal items, too, the things she'd brought in order to stay overnight with him?

Suddenly Joe went rigid, his hands resting on the back of a dining room chair, his head bowed. She waited.

Finally he spoke. ''So. You have your answers.''

''Yes.'' The word echoed in her chest, hollow now. ''My father was shot by his mistress's jealous boyfriend—former boyfriend. It was planned. A cold-blooded murder.''

''Do you wish you'd never gone searching for the truth?''

''I was asking myself that on the way here. I don't know how I feel about that yet.'' She moved closer to him. He straightened, almost backing away. ''How about you?''

"I don't have answers, only more questions."

"Yes." She put a hand on his arm, like touching steel. "What will you do?"

"I will wonder forever if my father was involved in a cover-up, as it appears."

She was so glad she hadn't told him about her mother and his father. Glad he wouldn't be burdened with that, too.

"You probably need to get to your office," he said, pulling back.

She decided he needed time to come to terms with what he'd learned. "I do," she said, then hesitated a few seconds. "Should I come back after work?"

He nodded.

She moved close to him. His eyes were vacant. She framed his face with her hands and kissed him softly. "Bye."

"Bye."

She took a few steps then turned back, an ache settling around her heart. "It happened a long time ago, Joe."

"Yeah."

If the situation were reversed she wouldn't want him trying to pacify her, so she left him to deal with the first blows alone, as she would want for herself. But the office was the last place she wanted to be.

More amazing than that—for the first time in her life, she was in love.

Joe stood in the dining room for several minutes after Arianna left. First he watched her car drive off. Then a slow-motion replay ran through his head. She'd kissed him goodbye.

He pulled up a chair and sat. What did it mean? She'd resisted kissing him hello and goodbye until now, and he hadn't known why. Now he was just as confused by the fact that she had kissed him.

In sympathy? Probably. Likely, he decided.

His cell phone rang. He roused himself to pull it from his pocket, but didn't recognize the caller's number listed on the tiny screen. "Joe Vicente," he said, striving for a normal voice.

"This is Paloma Clemente. Your lieutenant gave me your number. I'm very sorry to bother you, but I need to speak to my daughter."

Joe massaged the bridge of his nose as he made the mental adjustment from coming to terms with what he'd learned—and not learned—about his father, and the reality of speaking with Arianna's mother. "She's not here, Mrs Clemente. I imagine you can get her on her cell, though."

"I've been trying for days. She doesn't answer. I leave messages she doesn't return."

"Give her time."

"My daughter doesn't forgive and forget easily. If I don't push, she'll keep me out of her life for a much longer period of time."

He didn't want to get in the middle of the mother-daughter battle. "I don't know what to tell you."

"You're probably angry at me, too."

He heard something in her voice—resignation or apology, he didn't know which. "Angry?"

"Because of my relationship with your father. I'm sorry. Truly sorry."

Her relationship with his father?

"Please ask Arianna to call me, if you will. I'd really appreciate it. Goodbye."

His arm hit the table hard, his cell phone smacking the wood. Her relationship with his father? What the hell did she mean by that? And she'd said it in a way that had to mean Arianna knew, and that Paloma assumed Arianna had told him.

Her relationship with his father?

Dove. Joe sat up. Paloma meant dove. Her husband, Estebán, had even called her that, Joe remembered suddenly. He'd been too focused on Arianna that afternoon, on her reaction to what she was learning about her father.

Dove. He'd seen the word in his father's notebook.

He grabbed the papers then searched through his own index of the shorthand his father had used. Dove—the word was found on several pages, starting about a week after the murder. Before that, she was identified as P.A., for Paloma Alvarado.

He read it all, the references to P.A. and to "dove." The subtle shift from the cop's widow to woman.

Flames torched his stomach, crept up his esophagus. More deceit. More lies. His father and Arianna's mother. He had cheated, just as Jane had implied.

And Arianna knew. He'd praised her honesty, had valued it. And she'd been lying all along. Surely she'd seen the references to "dove" in the notes and known it was her mother.

It hurt more than Jane giving him back his ring. That, at least, had been honest. This was deception at its worst, playing on his emotions, not giving him credit for being able to deal with the truth. Making independent decisions that affected him. Not honoring him and his right to know, as if he were a child.

And by the woman he'd already placed above any other he'd known.

Seventeen

Arianna was usually the first one in the office every day and the last one to leave. Today, even though she was hours late, she didn't rush from the parking lot but strolled instead, hearing birdsong more than traffic and smelling the crispness of the day, not exhaust.

"Good morning," Arianna said to the receptionist, Julie. What she wanted to say was, I'm in love! Can you believe that? Me? In love?

"Good *afternoon*," Julie teased as she handed Arianna a stack of messages.

She smiled. "Are Nate and Sam in?"

"Nate's out of the office until after lunch. Sam called a while ago to say his plane was delayed, but he'll be here by—" she looked at her watch "—well, anytime now."

"Thanks." Arianna thumbed through the messages as she made her way to her office, saying good morning to people but not engaging in conversation. One of the messages was from Doc.

She was dialing his number before she'd even settled at her desk. "I hope you're ready to make a deal," she said after he answered.

"Maybe."

She smiled at the enigmatic response. She would enjoy working with him. "What do we need to do to entice you?"

"I want a partnership."

Disappointment twisted inside her as tightly as the phone cord she fingered. "That's not an option. Sam, Nate and I worked too hard to build ARC to give up part of the control to someone else. As you suggested on Saturday, I'd be willing to pay a bonus."

"There isn't a bonus big enough to cover the client base I'd be bringing. I'm e-mailing you the list right now. Take a look at it. I think the revenue is worth a partnership."

She booted her computer, waited as it loaded.

"Anything else you require?" she asked, although resigned to not having him come aboard.

"I don't want to be responsible for the day-to-day operations of the office, but I'd be willing to hire the other investigators you want."

"Do you have anyone in mind?" She typed a few keystrokes, connecting to her e-mail.

"Cassie Miranda. She's an in-house investigator for Oberman, Steele and Jenkins, a big law firm in the city. We should lure her. She's good. Damn good. And James Paladin. He was a bounty hunter for a long time, but gave it up recently. You'd be lucky to get him."

She pulled up the client list, scanned it, and sat back in awe, then clicked on the print button to make a copy. Politicians, celebrities and executives to rival ARC's extensive and exclusive list. Doc didn't talk through her silence. "What's your real name?"

He laughed. "Does that mean we have a deal?"

"I have to talk to Nate and Sam before I can make the offer."

"Okay. How'd things work out with your father's case?"

"When you're on board, I'll tell you," she said with a smile, reminded of her trip to San Francisco with Joe just two days ago. Only two days ago. She hadn't known she was in love then. If she had, she might have tried to convince him to spend the night in one of the world's most romantic cities.

Then they wouldn't have had Sunday free, and time to go to the Lakers game, and for Joe to see Jane, which he still hadn't told Arianna—

"Deal," Doc said, pulling her back into the conversation.

"I'll get back to you, probably later today," she said. She heard voices from outside her office and looked out her open door but saw nothing.

"My name's Quinn Gerard," Doc said.

"A perfectly respectable name. Why are you called Doc?" The noise from the outer office increased, but she still couldn't see a reason for it.

"You can't go in there!" she heard Abel Metzger, her biggest, burliest investigator, bellow.

"I'll tell you some other time," Doc said. "Talk to you later."

She said goodbye and hung up, standing at the same time, and heading for her door.

Joe found his path to Arianna's office blocked by a huge guy with an attitude.

"Call him off," Joe said when he spotted Arianna.

"Let him go, Abel," she said to the hulk. "It's okay."

Joe moved around him and went toward Arianna. She let him in then shut the door. He passed her a grocery bag filled with the things she'd left at his house. She glanced inside, paused, then set the bag on her desk, the motion deliberate, her face schooled. He knew that look. She was gathering her defenses.

"What's going on?" she asked, not able to hide her hurt completely.

Hurt. As if *she* should be the one hurting.

"Why didn't you tell me someone else played the sex card?"

Her face went blank for a moment, then something flashed in her eyes before she looked at the floor. Dammit. He'd hoped he'd been wrong. Hoped— *Dammit, Arianna. I can't believe you didn't tell me. I can't believe it.*

"You talked to my mother," she said, finally making eye contact.

"She called right after you left, looking for you. I guess you're not returning her calls."

"Let's sit down."

"To hell with sitting down. When were you going to tell me? Ever?" The words scraped his throat like sandpaper. He'd learned to trust her, and now… "My father and your mother? You didn't think I deserved to know?"

"I thought you had enough to deal with."

Disbelief chiseled a wedge into his anger, widening it, deepening it. "You think you have the right to make that kind of decision for me?"

She hitched a shoulder defensively. "Their relationship never went anywhere. It was an *infatuation.*" She pounded the word, emphasizing it. "An infatuation. One my mother took advantage of in her grief. Your father got protective of her—and me. She used his feelings to get him to declare my father's case unsolved so that I would remember him as a hero, not as someone who'd cheated on my mother and gotten himself killed because of it." Her voice had picked up volume and speed. She put out a hand as if she were going to touch him, then changed her mind.

He was glad. He didn't want her to touch him.

"She said your father fell in love with her," she continued, although in a quieter, slower voice, getting control of her emotions, keeping him from seeing anything below the surface. "And she used that love or whatever it was—which was despicable of her—but nothing happened between them."

"You couldn't have explained that to me?"

"I was trying to do you a favor."

"A *favor?*" He laughed harshly. "By not providing me with one of the key pieces of evidence?"

She frowned. "I don't know what you mean."

He stared at her, stunned. She couldn't be that dense. According to this guy she was trying to hire, Doc, she had the logic skills of a man. He'd seen it for himself. "Who do you suspect killed your father's killer?" he asked.

"Fred Zamora, as revenge," she said as if it were obvious.

He crossed his arms, waiting for her to elaborate. She didn't. "How do you figure that?"

"Because my father and Rollie were both killed with my father's police revolver. Zamora is the common denominator. He hunted down Rollie, probably trapped him, got the gun away from him and killed him with it."

"Cold-blooded murder?"

She shifted feet, obviously uncomfortable. "Maybe. Maybe they struggled. I don't know. What's your point?"

He was working hard at staying calm. "Who else could've killed Rollie?"

She half sat on her desk and rubbed her forehead. "He wasn't exactly one of the good guys. Probably any number of the creeps he hung around with, and who would've had access to the gun."

"True. Or my father." There. He'd said what had driven him there. The truth that had swept Joe into a whirlwind the moment he learned about his father's relationship with her mother. The secret relationship that Arianna had kept from him—him, the person with the most right to know.

She jerked away from the desk, her mouth open but no sound coming out. She shook her head over and over. "No. He wouldn't, Joe. He couldn't."

He tried to sort through her expression and her tone of voice. She hadn't considered it? But she *should* have. And she should have let him consider it. "Why not?" he asked. "He fell in love with her. Maybe he told her he knew who'd killed your father. Maybe she used my father for more than just getting the case sealed. Maybe she got him to kill. In fact, logically he's the most obvious suspect." He ground out the words that destroyed him to say out loud. How could anyone believe their own father was a killer?

He pounded a fist against his chest, as if his heart needed to be jump-started from the shock of the idea, then he pressed her again, harder. "By you withholding the fact that my father was in love with your mother, you denied me access to all of the evidence, denied me the ability to find the truth."

Arianna shook her head. Gone was the cool, controlled woman. In her place stood a different Arianna, one who looked a little frantic and desperate.

"Why not?" Joe asked. *Give me a reason to believe I'm wrong. Please, give me a reason.*

"Because sealing a case is one thing. Killing? I can't believe it."

Not good enough. ''I couldn't believe he would be involved in a cover-up, but he was. Why not more that that?''

''You can't compare the two. You can't.'' She took a
few steps away from him, her body rigid, then she hurried
back and grabbed his arms, demanding his attention. ''My
mother wouldn't have asked it of him, either.''

There it is. She just didn't want to believe her mother
capable of using someone for her own purposes. ''People
are capable of all sorts of things you wouldn't believe. That
was evidence you withheld. You make or break cases based
on evidence. *Evidence.* The gun was in my father's safe.''
It all made sense. And it hurt. ''And then there's the other
piece of evidence you decided not to tell me about. Why
didn't you tell me about 'dove'?''

Her brows drew together. ''I don't know what you're
talking about.''

''The connection of your mother's name, Paloma, to the
word dove, which shows up in my father's notes.''

''Where? I never saw that.''

''She's mentioned several times.''

Something in her changed then. She dropped her hands
and took a step back. A light went out in her eyes. Her
giving up got to him more than her defensiveness. He
wanted her to battle him on this, to tell him he was wrong,
to make him believe it.

''I did not see it,'' she said without emotion. ''But I'll
reread the notes. Maybe there are answers there.''

''I doubt it.''

Another transformation came over her, slowly, agoniz-
ingly, bleakly. Then ice frosted her expression, turning her
pale, taking away any trace of the fire he loved about her.
''So, you have tried and convicted me.''

When she put it like that he realized what a mistake he'd

made. A huge one. He started to speak, but she wouldn't let him, stepping over his words.

"You accused me early in this relationship of using the sex card, and now you accuse my mother. We are one and the same to you."

The truth snaked through him, past his shock and hurt, and coiled around his heart, squeezing hard. Uncertainty reared up. "I don't know what to believe."

"You could believe me. Have a little faith in me." She drew herself up proudly. "I never played the sex card," she said, cold and clear and strong. "Never. And I shouldn't have to defend myself, but I'm going to, so there are no misunderstandings. Yes, I sort of tricked you into meeting me, but I wasn't using sex—" she said the word harshly, accusingly "—to get you to do anything. What happened between us was mutual and totally out of my control—and yours, I think."

She barely stopped for a breath. "Second, I know I told you we wouldn't sleep together again after that first night, then I came to you anyway—but again, because I couldn't stop myself. I wasn't playing a game with you. I'd always had control over every relationship I'd been in before. I didn't know how to handle the loss of control. Maybe I made a few mistakes because of it."

"I—"

"Just listen. You owe me that much." She seemed like herself again—strong and majestic. "I've avoided cops as potential partners all of my adult life because I know they generally don't deal well with emotion," she said, moving close, getting in his face. "I should've avoided you, obviously, but I thought you were different. I even became protective of you, wanting to take care of you when no one else had for a long time. To help you heal."

Her eyes filled with fury, devastating in its truth, which

he was just beginning to see. He should've asked questions, not made accusations. The price he would pay for his mistake could be enormous. How could he fix it? How could he settle things down so they could figure out what to do next?

"Arianna—"

"How dare you accuse me of doing what my mother did." Her anger filled the room like a snarling monster. "She used your father's infatuation for her own purposes. I never used you. I worked with you. I made love with you. I gave you more of myself than I've given anyone. Ever. And what do you do? You throw it back at me, saying I lied. Maybe there's a fine line between withholding the truth and lying. Maybe you think I crossed it. But so did you."

"I—" He stopped. "When?"

"First, when you didn't tell me your parents wouldn't be at their house when I said I wanted to come there."

"I was curious why—"

"That's crap." She waved a hand. "You could have—should have—told me. And, second, yesterday you had a conversation with your ex-fiancée at the Lakers game, a conversation that upset you. Not only did you not tell me about it, you denied anything was wrong when I outright asked you about it."

He'd forgotten about it. Ridiculous. He'd forgotten. "You saw?"

"And I waited, giving you space to deal with it, because I knew if I joined you, it would stop the conversation, one that apparently needed to take place. Don't you think it hurt me that you didn't share that? But I tried to understand. I was willing to wait. I assumed you would tell me eventually, if it mattered." She faltered, made a sound of frustration, then turned her back on him. "I can't believe how wrong I was about you."

She grabbed her purse off her desk and headed for the door, where she stopped and turned around. Her eyes were bright. Tears? Because of him? Idiot, he called himself. Stupid idiot.

"Arianna—"

She stopped him with a look he couldn't describe, a combination of hurt and distance, as if she'd already separated herself from him.

"One of the reasons I didn't tell you about my mother and your father," she said with heat, "was because I didn't want to put you in the position of seeing my mother for the rest of your life and knowing that about her. It didn't occur to me that your father would kill for her. Not once. If I'd realized it was evidence, *I would've told you.*" Her voice shook. She swiped a hand over her cheeks, pushing away tears. "But mostly—" she stopped, took a breath as another tear trailed down her face, then another "—mostly I didn't tell you because I didn't want to damage your image of your father any more than it already had been. He can't defend himself, can he?" She opened the door. "Goodbye. It's been…an experience."

Joe stared after her, too shell-shocked to move. His throat convulsed. He couldn't even call out to her to stay. Lieutenant Morgan had been right, after all, when he'd worried that Joe would get hurt—or someone else would. He'd blown up. Stupidly. So totally unlike him. And she was right—by withholding truths from her, he'd done the same thing she had, maybe not even for reasons as good as she had.

She hadn't done what her mother did. Not even close. He'd jumped to conclusions because of what Jane had told him yesterday—that his father had cheated on his mother.

Added to what Paloma had said on the phone about her having a relationship with his father… He'd made assumptions. A man in his profession should know better than to make assumptions.

A few of her parting words struck him then. She hadn't wanted to put him in the position of seeing her mother for the rest of his life? Meaning she'd expected him to be in her life forever? As in marriage?

This morning she'd kissed him goodbye for the first time.

He slammed his fist into the door. "Dammit!" How could he have been so blind? He'd been as afraid of the truth as she had been, yet she'd faced it better, more honestly.

He needed to catch her before she—

"You've worn out your welcome," Sam Remington said, blocking his way.

Joe looked past Sam to the windows overlooking the parking lot. He saw Arianna's car pull out, heard rubber squeal. "I've got to stop her."

Sam didn't move. "Seems to me you made a whole lot of mistakes."

"I recognize that now. We both did." But that didn't mean it was over. He looked Sam in the eye, wondering about his protectiveness. "I won't hurt her again."

"See that you don't." Sam moved aside.

Joe raced to the parking lot then realized he didn't even know where she lived. He tried calling her cell phone. She didn't answer. He glanced at the building, saw Sam watching him and knew he wouldn't be welcome at her office again. He didn't know where she took yoga classes or tae kwon do or which shooting range she used. Where did that leave him?

Between a rock and a hard place.

Well, hell, even between a rock and a hard place, sunlight could get through. He just needed to follow the light.

Eighteen

It was rare for Joe to work on a Saturday night, but here he was, scanning a large crowd of starstruck fans all hoping for a glimpse of their favorite celebrity. The event was a charity ball to benefit an animal rescue group, a popular cause among the entertainment crowd. Ironically, Joe was there because one of the guests, the CEO of a pharmaceutical company, had been targeted by a small, radical organization protesting the use of lab animals in pharmaceutical testing.

Trevor Hollings, the CEO, was assaulted at a similar event two months ago, the worst of his injuries caused by pepper spray in his eyes. Tonight everyone would've preferred he enter the grand hotel through a different entrance, but he refused, even though he was putting other people in harm's way just to prove he couldn't be cowed.

Normally, the event planners would hire off-duty cops for security. This time the department sent officers, having been tipped that the protest would get uglier than the last one. The information was deemed reliable enough that Joe and his partner, Tony Mendes, were preassigned to do the follow-up and build a criminal case, if necessary. Instead of waiting at home for a call, Joe and Mendes decided to attend, the threat viable enough to make it worth their time.

Plus, Joe had nothing better to do on a Saturday night. He'd returned to work after begging his lieutenant to cut short his forced vacation. He'd done as much as humanly possible to get Arianna to talk to him. Sent flowers to her office, bombarded her with e-mails. One time he dared to be in the parking lot waiting for her to arrive at work, but she'd driven in, seen him, and driven out.

How the hell was he supposed to win her back if he couldn't get near her? It wasn't like she was going to call him. The only communication he'd received was one short e-mail, in which she said she'd read his father's pages looking for "dove." She'd found the references, all right, but that he should know she'd thought his father had written "done," his writing hard to read, as Joe well knew. She'd told Joe to go back and read them, substituting the word "done," and see that it made sense, too, that she hadn't lied. She'd never seen it.

He hadn't even looked at the notes to verify it. He believed her. Then he'd stopped trying to contact her. She was more stubborn than he was. Unless she was willing to meet him halfway, there was no way he could make amends.

The noisy crowd brought Joe back to the present and the job he was there to do. He hung with the crowd on the right side of the red carpet, watching. Mendes mingled on the other side. The uniforms created space between the celebrities and fans, and took heat for blocking the view.

Joe read the handmade signs poking above the crowd

here and there. Some appealed to a certain star to look their
way, but political statements also dotted the landscape, the
usual hot topics, minus one—animal rights, glaring in its
omission.

He looked for backpacks, jackets with big pockets, tote
bags. Gloves would be out of place on this unusually warm
November evening, and could indicate someone about to
handle sharp metal or glass—or even acid. Unfortunately
backpacks were in vogue, so they were everywhere.

"Head's up," he heard in his earpiece. "Next car is
Hollings's."

Joe scoped the crowd, watching for a shift. The limo
pulled up. The driver came around to the passenger side
and opened the door. A red high heel emerged, then an
ankle. A slender calf. A few spectacular inches of thigh,
revealed by a long slit in the dress. The rest of the incredible body followed, clothed in body-hugging red, the
beaded fabric sparkling. A deep V exposed a tempting
amount of cleavage. Diamonds shimmered at her throat.
Her head emerged, dark hair pulled back and coiled low,
like a certain flamenco dancer he remembered. Red lipstick.
A small beauty mark near her mouth that he couldn't see
but knew was there.

Arianna.

Hollings's private security.

Arianna was relieved to be getting out of the limo. Her
fifty-two-year-old "date" and client, Trevor Hollings, wore
an elegant yet trendy tuxedo. He had striking salt-and-
pepper hair and a toned body that men twenty years
younger would envy—and women would covet. He was
flirtatious and charming.

Too bad he was also boring and egotistical.

A minute ago, as the car had pulled into the line of others

dropping off passengers, she'd said to Hollings, "I need to stay on your right side. Take your cues from me. If I touch you, let me, but don't touch me back. Don't hold my hand or do anything that might prevent me from protecting you."

"All right."

"If someone runs toward us, don't try to help me. Let me do my job."

"That's why I hired you."

She'd pointed out the window. "Take a look at the faces. Tell me if you see anyone familiar."

After a bit he said, "They all kind of blend together. Just bodies. And lots of cops."

An unusually large number, Arianna thought as she scanned the scene.

"I guess he was serious," Hollings said.

"Who?"

"The detective who called today saying he thought there might be trouble tonight."

Arianna counted to three, all she had time for. "You didn't think that was information I needed?"

"I'm not afraid."

Idiot. "There's a difference between fear and preparation. I would've added more people."

"I didn't want more. And I did tell him I had hired security."

She wouldn't work for him again.

"I'll precede you from the car," she said, checking her anger. "We're walking quickly and directly into the hotel. Got it?"

He nodded. She didn't believe him. She was rarely wrong about someone, but she'd thought when she met him last month that he was sensible and intelligent. Her mistake. One she hoped wouldn't cost her.

Cameras flashed, almost blinding her as she stepped out

of the limo. Expectation buzzed in the air, but diminished as Hollings emerged and the crowd and the paparazzi realized they weren't celebrities of the movie-star type. The flashes stopped. She scanned the crowd. Four men and a woman pushed through a gap in the police line.

"Move in! Move in!" she heard a man yell, someone familiar—

She shoved Hollings toward a uniformed officer. "Get him inside," she ordered, absorbing the blow of something heavy and metal against her shoulder, but keeping her hands on Hollings's back, pushing him from behind.

The events unfolded in seconds. The five protestors were joined by others from the other side and moved as a unit, tossing bottles, cans and sticks at Hollings—and Arianna—as they hurried along the carpet, jammed now with protestors and police. Arianna stayed at Hollings's back. She was showered with objects that scratched and scraped and punctured her skin. Fury spurred her to turn around just as two men got close enough to use pepper spray. She kicked the canisters out of their hands, connecting hard, immobilizing them. Their agonizing cries filled the air. "Bitch!" one yelled, gripping his damaged hand. Like she cared.

Officers tackled the men, knocking one into her. She tripped over him just as Hollings disappeared safely into the building. The man on the ground clutched a metal stake. There was no way to reverse her body's direction, no way to stop her fall. She put out a hand to try to deflect it—

She was yanked back. Her rescuer landed hard on the ground, rolling as he hit, acting as a cushion, absorbing the blow. Air whooshed out of her lungs. She couldn't move, could barely breathe.

"Are you okay?" the man asked, harsh and low.

Joe. Oh, God. *Joe.*

His grip loosened. He sat up, taking her with him.

"Are you okay?" he repeated, more harshly.

"I'm okay." She tried to look at him but couldn't turn around far enough. She saw that the police had gotten control of the protestors. "What are you doing here?"

"Same as you. My job." He set his hands on her waist and pulled her up as he stood. "Let me see your shoulder."

She faced away from him, felt his fingers graze her skin. She closed her eyes. She'd missed him. Missed him so much. Every hour of every day. Every minute of every night. Every second of every dream. It had been so hard to resist his notes and flowers, but she had a hard time believing he could have made the mental shift from believing they couldn't ever get past the strangeness of their history. Her mother was still alive. After what Paloma had done, how could Joe ever have a relationship with her?

Pride and worry had bitten Arianna then wouldn't let go. She didn't know how to make up with someone. She'd never had to before.

And apparently she'd been right. He'd stopped trying to contact her.

"You're going to have a bruise the size of Texas." He skimmed other spots. "You need these looked at and cleaned. You're bleeding. You'll need a tetanus shot."

She turned toward him and noted how his eyes shone with dark, unnamed emotion. Suddenly she couldn't come up with any good reason why she'd kept him at bay. They'd both made mistakes. She could take the first step toward making up. "Thank you."

His mouth tightened as if he were furious at her. She didn't know what to think. Then he called over an officer. "Take her inside," he said. "Someone will be in to take her statement, then she needs to go to the hospital."

He turned away, leaving her standing there with her mouth open, watching him, feeling dismissed. Was he angry that she'd gotten caught up in the violence? There'd been an edge to his voice when he'd said that he was doing his job, same as she was. He didn't think a woman should be in the protection business?

She checked on Hollings, who was amazingly unscathed, gave her statement to a detective named Mendes, waited about an hour, then she left, angry and humiliated that he'd ignored her. Her address was on her statement. He could find her when—if—he was ready.

Now or never, she thought. An ending or a new beginning. *The ball's in your court, Joe.*

Joe broke speed limits to get to his father's care facility at eight-thirty the next morning. He should be at the office. He still had hours of paperwork ahead of him. But Mrs. Winters had called to say Arianna was with his father.

Until yesterday he had no idea Arianna had been coming to visit him, almost every day. Joe had found out only because she'd left behind a sweater. He'd picked it up and smelled her perfume. When he'd asked Mrs. Winters she said she'd been sworn to secrecy.

It was a secret no longer.

He jogged up the walkway, let himself in, then rushed down the hall and into his father's room, coming to an abrupt stop. Chief barked once before he recognized Joe then wagged his tail. His father and Arianna looked up from the table where they sat peacefully cutting out pictures from magazines and gluing them onto sheets of paper.

"Where have you been?" Joe demanded of her, relief sweeping through him at the same time. He made a quick visual check of her. She looked fine.

She glanced at his father, at the startled look on his face, then frowned pointedly at Joe. "I've been right here," she said cheerfully.

There was a bite to her words, however. He ran a hand down his face, exhausted, but more than ready to spar with her, anything to have an outlet for the rush of emotion now that he knew she was all right, except that his father responded well only to tranquility and routine. Joe was supplying neither. He knew better than to bring problems into his father's room.

"You were supposed to wait for me," he said as calmly as possible. "No one knew where you were. I called every hospital. You didn't check in."

"You did not say to wait for you, but I did, anyway—for an hour. Then I called my own doctor. She met me at her office. I'm fine." She smiled, although not a true one. "Come look at the collage that Mike is making. Isn't it great?"

His father smiled like a child stuck between arguing parents. Joe let out a slow breath and moved closer.

"You sent your *partner* to interview me," she said, an undertone of irritation in her voice.

"That's great, Dad." Joe patted his father's back and looked at Arianna. "I knew Mendes would be impartial and unemotional. I couldn't guarantee that I could be. Plus, I was in charge. I was busy."

"It would've taken thirty seconds, a minute, tops, to come see me."

"I wouldn't have wanted to leave." Could he be any more direct?

"You stopped sending me flowers."

Ah. Was that the problem? He'd stopped pursuing her? Had she expected he would keep at it forever?

He couldn't continue this discussion in front of his father, who looked increasingly confused and agitated. "Can we talk about it later? I need to get back to work."

She didn't look at him. After a moment she got up and

left the room, just like that. No warning. No goodbye. Nothing. She'd grabbed her purse, so he assumed she was leaving for good.

Joe didn't know what to think.

Chief started to follow, perhaps picking up on her mood. "Chief. Stay," his father said. The dog obeyed.

Joe went still. Chief? He'd called the dog Chief, not Sarge? He stared at his father, seeing rare lucidity staring back. "Dad?"

"Better go after her, son."

He hesitated a couple of seconds, then knelt in front of his father, his father who recognized him for the first time in ages. Maybe the last time. Joe hugged him tight, felt his father's arms around him as if for the first time. "I love you, Dad."

"I love you, too." His father kissed his cheek. "Go after her," he repeated.

Joe couldn't. It would mean giving up his chance to ask about the murder, and his father's role in what happened after. Maybe the only time he could get answers.

Arianna would understand why he didn't go after her. He knew that.

He closed his eyes. Did he really want the answers? Wasn't it better to give it up, to stop obsessing about it, to let it go, and find a new passion? A life? A *happy* life.

"I'll be back, Dad." He hugged his father again then left the room at a run, flung open the front door.

Arianna was sitting on the stoop.

"Took you long enough," she said, her voice shaking.

He didn't tell her why. She would insist they go back inside and ask the questions. The answers didn't matter anymore.

He sat beside her, not quite close enough to touch, but almost.

"Why have you been coming to see my father?" he asked, looking straight ahead.

"He was kind to me years ago. Truly kind. My mother shouldn't have—" She stopped. "I just needed to be with him. Okay?"

"Okay." He looked at her then, his heart in his throat. She was kind, too. "Did you miss me?" he asked quietly.

She met his gaze. Finally she nodded.

"You can't say it?" he persisted.

"You first."

He wanted to laugh. Instead he said, "I missed you."

"Me, too."

He wove his fingers with hers. "I wasn't ignoring you last night. When I saw you about to get hurt, your life passed before my eyes. It twisted me up inside so much I could hardly think. All I wanted to do was carry you away and take care of you. The thought of you hurt…"

She leaned against him. He kissed her hair. His eyes stung.

"I had to do my job. I couldn't do that and take care of you at the same time."

"I know," she said. "I was being selfish. After it was over and I realized how close I came to—" She stopped. "I didn't know what to do. I'm so used to handling everything alone, but I wanted you to be with me. To take care of me. That was a first. I thought it was a weakness, so I ran away. I'm sorry I scared you."

"Don't do it again."

She laughed a little. "I won't."

He pulled her into his arms. "I love you."

"I love you, too," she said in a voice he hadn't heard before. One filled with tenderness and relief and ferocity.

Then he kissed her. The first kiss of a lifetime. There would be plenty more—good-morning and good-night kisses, passionate ones, tender ones. Make-up kisses, we're-going-to-have-a-baby kisses, the-baby-looks-like-you kisses. And so many more.

But this one was the most special.

"Let's go see your father," she said after a while.

He nodded, wondering which father would greet them, but knowing that either one would be okay. Everything was going to be okay.

*   *   *   *   *

Silhouette®

Desire

DYNASTIES : THE DANFORTHS

A family of prominence...
tested by scandal, sustained by passion.

COWBOY CRESCENDO
(Silhouette Desire #1591)

by Cathleen Galitz

Newly hired nanny Heather Burroughs quickly
won over Toby Danforth's young son with her
warmth and humor, but Toby's affection was
harder to tap into. This sizzling cowboy was
still reeling from his disastrous divorce and
certainly wasn't looking for a new bride.
Could Heather lasso this lone rancher
and get him to settle down?

*Available July 2004
at your favorite retail outlet.*

COMING NEXT MONTH

#1591 COWBOY CRESCENDO—Cathleen Galitz
Dynasties: The Danforths
Newly hired nanny Heather Burroughs quickly won over Toby Danforth's young son with her warmth and humor, but Toby's affection was harder to tap into. This sexy cowboy was still reeling from his disastrous divorce and wasn't looking to involve himself in any type of relationship. Could Heather lasso this lone rancher into settling down?

#1592 BEST-KEPT LIES—Lisa Jackson
The McCaffertys
Green-eyed P.I. Kurt Striker was hired to protect Randi McCafferty and her baby against a mysterious attacker. After being run off the road by this veiled villain, Randi had the strength to survive any curve life threw her. But did she have the power to steer clear of her irresistibly rugged protector?

#1593 MISS PRUITT'S PRIVATE LIFE—Barbara McCauley
Secrets!
Brother to the groom Evan Carter was immediately attracted to friend of the bride and well-known television personality Marcy Pruitt. While helping to pull the wedding together, they found themselves falling into a scandalous affair. But when Miss Pruitt's private life became public knowledge, would their shared passion result in a wedding of their own?

#1594 STANDING OUTSIDE THE FIRE—Sara Orwig
Stallion Pass: Texas Knights
Former Special Forces colonel and sexy charmer Boone Devlin clashed with Erin Frye over the ranch she managed and he had recently inherited. The head-to-head confrontation soon turned into head-over-heels passion. This playboy made it clear that nothing could tame him—but could an unexpected pregnancy change that?

#1595 BABY AT *HIS* CONVENIENCE—Kathie DeNosky
She wanted a strong, sexy man to father her child—and waitress Katie Andrews had decided that Jeremiah Gunn fit the bill exactly. Trouble was, Jeremiah had some terms of his own before he'd agree to give Katie what she wanted…and that meant becoming his mistress….

#1596 BEYOND CONTROL—Bronwyn Jameson
Free-spirited Kree O'Sullivan had never met a sexier man than financier Sebastian Sinclair. Even his all-business, take-charge attitude intrigued her. Just once she wanted Seb to go wild—for her. But when the sizzling attraction between them began to loosen *her* restraints, she knew passion would soon spiral out of control…for both of them.

SDCNM0604